AFTER ST BRIDE

Also by Marcus Attwater

The Chapter of St Cloud
St Oda's Bones
The Gift
The Secrets of Greystone House
Scottish Baronial

AFTER ST BRIDE

MARCUS ATTWATER

ISBN: 9798327734685
Copyright © Marcus Attwater 2024
Cover design by Attwater Books. Photograph: Shutterstock

www.attwaterbooks.nl

The Farndales of Ulvercott House

Victor Farndale
Olivia Westmacott, Victor's first wife *(deceased)*
    Robert Farndale, Victor and Olivia's son
    Bettina McKinley, Robert's wife
        Oliver Farndale, Robert and Bettina's son
        Poppy Alexander, Oliver's fiancée
        Bella Farndale, Robert and Bettina's daughter
    Elinor (Nora) Farndale, Victor and Olivia's daughter
    Sunita Mahajan, Nora's partner
Annabel Rokeby, Victor's second wife *(deceased)*
    Electra Farndale, Victor and Annabel's daughter
    Matt Fielding, Electra's fiancé
    Antigone Farndale, Victor and Annabel's daughter
    Simon Danvers, Antigone's boyfriend
    Mortimer Farndale, Victor and Annabel's son
Eliza Sanford, Victor's third wife
    David Farndale, Victor and Eliza's son
Ursula Westmacott, Olivia's sister
    Juliette Westmacott, Olivia and Ursula's niece

1

It was one of those still winter days when the park looks like a film set, the sky so pale that it was almost white. The house was silent as well, although I knew there must be people around somewhere. Jacqueline was probably in the kitchen, too far away to hear the creak as I went up the wooden stairs. There was no one about on the first floor, and the old man was in his room, watching television. I could hear the opening tune of Sherlock *– he has always liked clever people who are also a bit weird. I found the dispensing tray where it always is, in the cabinet in his dressing room. The lid opened with a click that sounded loud to me, but he couldn't have heard it over the sound of the TV. There were pink capsules in there, and the little white pills I was looking for. They looked even more like the ones I had brought with me than I'd hoped, and I was sure no one would notice the difference. It was so easy to swap them, it hardly felt special. While Sherlock played his violin I put the box back where it belonged and slipped out of the room again, and back downstairs.*

I went out through the back, making a detour past the pond to approach the house again from the front. The bus had just dropped its passengers by the main gate, so with any luck it would look like I had only just arrived. Jacqueline opened the door for me when I rang the bell, and said everyone would be so glad to see me (although she says that to everybody who arrives at Ulvercott House). Now all I have to do is wait.

It was so *easy.*

2

When Owen Collins came downstairs on Monday morning, Dominic was at the kitchen table, reading the local paper on his laptop. They had bought the house in Flanders Alley in November and had been living together for just over a month, so this still felt quite new.

'Listen to this,' Dominic said, '*Parishioners of St Oda's church in Abbey Hill have voiced objections to the recent appointment of an openly gay rector. Mrs Barton (79) of Brook End expressed the opinion...* well, you can guess the rest. When they put it like that I always wonder if they'd be happier with a secretly gay rector.'

'Possibly they would.'

Owen recalled what he knew about St Oda's while he made coffee for himself (Dominic was a confirmed tea drinker). 'I really don't see what they are so worried about. They've had an accessory to murder, an alcoholic, an atheist and an adulterer in the past. Why would they object to an—' he ran down, unable to think of a suitable term starting with 'a'.

'Adam?' Dominic suggested, 'His name is Adam Rokeby.'

'Rokeby? That rings a bell. Is there a picture?'

Dominic looked at him over the top of his screen. 'No. But it does say he is 38 and single. Which, I may remind you, you are not.'

Owen sat down at the table with his coffee and toast. He rather liked being reminded. 'Anything else interesting?'

'There's an obituary of a Victor Farndale which presupposes I know all about him, but I've no idea who he is.'

'Ah, our local boy made good. A real rags to riches story, that: raised in St Bride's – the orphanage, you know – and went on to lead one of Britain's biggest software companies. Farndale Tech, even you must have heard of that. He wasn't that old, was he?'

'Seventy-two, but he'd been ill for a while, apparently. So it is his name on the museum?'

Dominic was due to give a lecture at the Farndale Museum later that month.

'Yes, he wasn't really one for conspicuous philanthropy, but without him we'd still have dusty cases and typewritten labels.'

The day went rather downhill from there. As soon as Collins arrived at the station, the desk sergeant told him that there had been another violent attack in the town centre. After the unprovoked assault on Sylvester Murray last week, they had all been hoping it would be a one-off, but apparently not. On Friday night another innocent passer-by had been beaten up by four men answering to the same description. Detective Inspector Graham was on the case.

Peter Graham had joined them at the start of the new year. He had been a DCI in Bournemouth, but he had been out of the running for nearly a year with a stress-related illness. Now he was recovering, and had returned to work as the Petergate station's second inspector. He was a conscientious copper in his early fifties, and Collins had taken to him at once. DC Josh Robbins, the youngest member of the team, also got on well with the new DI, and appeared to have decided that finally here was someone he could trust to teach him to be a good detective. It stung a little that Robbins clearly preferred working with Graham, but it wasn't surprising, really. Collins would be the first to admit that he could be idiosyncratic at times, and DS Sally Holmes didn't really have the patience to show someone the ropes. Now they made two good teams, with DS Pardoe and DC Dasgupta free to assist whoever needed them most. All the CID lacked now was a new boss, and DCI Flynn's successor was due to start that morning.

'I wonder if she's as passionate about punctuality as Bridget,' Collins said, as they assembled in the CID room.

'But you know DCI Dixon already, don't you? From your time in Oxford,' Sally asked.

Collins shook his head. 'No, she arrived after I left, I just missed her.'

'She can't have been there long then,' his colleague said thoughtfully.

'That doesn't have to mean anything.'

It was better not to speculate on why an officer was moved on within a year of arriving. DCI Dixon could have requested a transfer herself, or she had come up for promotion and they already had a full complement of CID officers. It didn't have to mean she'd done badly in her time at Oxford. Collins had virtuously resisted looking her up on Facebook when they had been told she would be stepping into Bridget's shoes, and hadn't even asked about her when he had called to congratulate his Oxford colleague DS Latimer on her promotion.

At nine exactly, DCI Rowena Dixon entered the CID room. She was a woman of about Collins's own age, wearing a tailored jacket over cream trousers, four-inch heels, and the kind of large black-framed glasses people wore to be seen with rather than see through. She didn't much look like a police officer, but then, who did?

'Good morning, everyone,' she said, with a wide smile, 'I'm DCI Rowena Dixon. Isn't everybody here yet? I was expecting the full team.'

Her new colleagues exchanged glances. Even Robbins knew that the Oxford station was three times the size of this one.

'This *is* the full team, ma'am,' Collins said, 'Except for DC Dasgupta, who is away on honeymoon. I'm DI Collins. This is DI Graham, who has been assigned to us temporarily, DS Pardoe, DS Holmes, and DC Robbins.'

DCI Dixon looked a little taken aback.

'All right. Well, I think you had better go on with the meeting as you normally would, so I can get an idea of how things are done here. Current cases?'

Collins, since he had apparently been elected spokesman, replied.

'Last week we finally caught the people behind a series of office thefts in the city, I'm processing the last evidence for that. Otherwise we have only one major investigation ongoing. Peter?'

DI Graham summarised the assault case to date for the DCI's benefit, and continued to inform them about the latest victim.

'Samir Khan, attacked in Minster Street in the early hours of Saturday morning. He's already given a statement, but he was a bit groggy, so I'm talking to him again today. I just hope he noticed more than Mr Murray did last week.'

The new DCI nodded. 'Fine. I assume all the relevant intel is in HOLMES? Right, then that's all for now. Of course I'll make time in the next few days to talk to each of you in turn so we can get to know each other better.'

She got up and went through to her office, closing the door behind her. The rest of the team sat and looked at each other, no one wanting to be the first to speak. Then Sally voiced what they were all thinking.

'It's a miracle she doesn't fall over in those heels.'

After the CID meeting Collins went into his office to tie up the last loose ends of his own case, but he had only just logged on when the desk sergeant called up that there was someone to see him.

'Says it's murder, sir.'

His colleague sounded sceptical, but Collins called Sally to sit in anyway. You never knew.

The man who came into his office was a few years younger than himself, around thirty, at a guess. He was tall and skinny, with untidy black hair, and dressed casually in jeans and a checked shirt.

'My name is Matt Fielding,' he said, shaking hands, 'Thank you for seeing me, Inspector. I assume you have heard of the death of Victor Farndale?'

Collins agreed that he had, and Mr Fielding sat down. 'Good, then I won't have to explain so much. His family believe he was murdered, you see. And they think I did it.'

He said this with a remarkable lack of flourish, and Collins did his best to match the businesslike tone.

'They do? You had better tell us everything, Mr Fielding.'

Sally came in with three coffees from the canteen, and Collins asked their visitor if he was all right with the conversation being recorded. These preliminaries out of the way, Mr Fielding launched into his story.

3

Matt

My name is Matt Fielding, I am 28 years old and I work as a geomorphologist at the University of Southampton. I am – I was – engaged to be married to Electra, Victor Farndale's daughter. I say 'was' because I had decided I could not go through with it. But we'll get to that.
Electra and I were to spend last weekend with her family at Ulvercott House, the manor house north of town, on the Newbury Road. It's where Electra's father lived with his third wife and their son, as well as Electra and her brother and sister from his second marriage. Electra's older siblings, her niece and nephew, and a cousin were also there for the weekend. They always got together on the anniversary of Victor's first wife's death, as they did on two or three other occasions throughout the year. Victor was raised in an orphanage, he knew nothing about his parents or where he came from, and that made it all the more important for him to have his own family around. That was something we had in common. since I also grew up in a home. I got along well with Electra's father, although we were very different in other respects.
Like most of the guests, I arrived on Friday. It was all much like other occasions when I had met Electra's family, as far as I could tell. No one did or said anything out of the ordinary. But perhaps I would not have noticed if they had. I was preoccupied because I had realised there was a reason I could not continue my relationship with Electra. She and her

twin sister Antigone were talking to their aunt, and they both said they did not want to have children of their own. I had always imagined us having a family, and I felt a bit let down. I think, in that moment, I didn't even like Electra very much. So all Friday and Saturday I was thinking of how best to tell her that I believed we'd better part.

Victor, Electra's father, was seventy-two years old, and not in great health. There was something wrong with his heart, and he took medication for that, but he gave no indication that he was feeling especially poorly this weekend. If anything, I thought he looked better, and happy to have all his children back at the house. Nonetheless, on Saturday evening, just after dinner, Victor suffered a fatal myocardial infarction.

His wife heard a noise from his room and found him unconscious there, half fallen from his bed. An ambulance was called, but the paramedics couldn't revive him. He was pronounced dead on arrival by a physician at the hospital. I believe there is to be a post-mortem, since the death was unexpected despite his condition.

Naturally we were all shocked and sad, and most of Sunday was spent talking about what had happened, and if anything could have been done to prevent it. Eliza wasn't there, she preferred to be alone, and so did David, her son. So this was Electra and me, her brother Robert and his wife and kids, her sisters with their partners, her aunt, and her cousin Juliette. And they were all talking about how they could have stopped their father dying. Victor was a rich man, he had the best medical care anyone could afford, and a nurse came to check on him several times a week, so I didn't see what more could have been done, and I said so. That was when I became aware that what had been meant – I think it was Antigone who brought it up – was whether anything could have been done to prevent someone killing Victor. It hadn't occurred to me at all that he could have been murdered. But as I said, he was rich, and almost everyone who was in the house at that time benefits financially from his death. Including myself, I suppose, if I did marry Electra. Still, it didn't seem to me to be a very likely scenario, and I was surprised that Victor's children and grandchildren all accepted it as possible, even likely. They thought someone had tampered with Victor's pills, substituted something lethal for his usual tablets. Not something we could easily verify, and surely a premature conclusion, but they all seemed quite convinced. They were discussing who had been alone with Victor on Friday or Saturday, and that's when I realised that I had, for quite some time on Saturday morning, been alone with him, and so had Simon, Antigone's boyfriend, but none of the others. And that was odd. Victor was not always well enough to spend the day downstairs, and he liked to see his family in his room one by one, where he could give them his undivided attention. But none of his offspring had gone in to see him on their own this time, only in pairs.

It was at this point that I started to become uneasy. I am not a fanciful person, but I think it is fair to say that Electra and her twin are, and I had the distinct impression that glances were being cast in my direction. They couldn't stop talking about it, and by the end of the afternoon they had quite convinced themselves that there was no doubt at all that Victor had been murdered, and it was only a question of time before they worked out by whom.

Robert – their half-brother, the eldest – wanted to call the police at once, but when his daughter Bella suggested that that would only make them all look suspicious he agreed to wait until after the post-mortem. I left shortly after that, and I have not spoken to any member of the family since. But I could not stop thinking about it. Electra and her siblings like to act conspiratorial, so there may be nothing in it. On the other hand, I also know that they are ruthless enough to hatch a plot and let someone else take the blame. And wouldn't an outsider make a perfect scapegoat? Perhaps Electra has come to the same conclusion as I did and just found a more radical way to end our relationship. I don't know. I really don't know. But I wanted to tell my own story first.

So that's it. I don't know whether Victor Farndale was murdered. It may be that the shock has brought on some collective delusion in Electra and her siblings, and there is nothing in it at all. But if he was murdered in the way they suppose, I am one of the people who definitely had the opportunity, and they are very much aware of it. If this becomes a murder inquiry, there will be fingers pointed at me. But I did not kill Victor. I am very sorry he is dead.

4

Early that afternoon, Sally Holmes was in the gym, hitting a punchbag so hard it was occasionally hitting her back. *Damn, damn, damn!* This wasn't her, this shouldn't be happening. She didn't get upset during interviews. She didn't get entangled with witnesses, that was Collie's department. She didn't let her past influence her work. Hell, she didn't let her past influence her life. And then the past had walked into the police station, all grown up and confident. He had recognised her at once, she was sure of it, and had decided not to complicate things by claiming acquaintance. Sensible, from his point of view. Matt had always been the sensible one. Now it was up to her, and she didn't know what to do.

Panting, she wiped the sweat from her brow with a boxing glove. Correction: she did know what to do, she just didn't want to do it. One thing was certain though, if she had to talk, she'd talk to Owen, and not to that shiny specimen headquarters had landed them with. Sally had never worked under any DCI expect Bridget Flynn, and hadn't realised until now how much she had relied on her quiet competence and straight talking. For that matter, DCI Flynn had already known some of what Sally had been— not *hiding*, never hiding, but definitely avoiding talking about.

Having pummelled both her anger and the punchbag into submission, DS Holmes showered, changed, and went to talk to her boss.

Victor Farndale, the obituary in the Messenger told Collins, had been born in 1942 to unknown parents, who had left him in the porch of the cathedral as a newborn. He had spent the first sixteen years of his life in St Bride's Orphanage on Fletcher Street.

A large Catholic orphanage throughout the first half of the twentieth century, in the seventies St Bride's had been transformed into a small scale children's home run by social services. Nowadays it was just a temporary facility for children waiting to be placed with a foster family. According to Mr Fielding, he had been among the last children to live there permanently. It was an odd coincidence, that Victor and his daughter's fiancé had both grown up in St Bride's. Could Victor's background still be relevant, after all those years?

After being educated at a technical training college, Victor joined a local electronics company as an engineer, but he was always more interested in the business side of things, and soon became an important figure in its marketing department. He was married for the first time in 1968, to Olivia Westmacott, the daughter of a judge, which was a measure of how far he had already travelled from his obscure origins. There were two children from the marriage, but his wife died in 1974. By that time Victor had set up his own company producing desktop calculators. Two years after he was widowed Farndale married a young actress, Annabel Rokeby, with whom he had a further three children.

In the early eighties Farndale Tech branched out into software engineering for the booming computer market. The company went from strength to strength, mainly because Farndale was never afraid to embrace new developments or team up with experts in other fields. In the late nineties Farndale Tech acquired a small video game design company which went on to develop the popular GrailQuest franchise. Widowed for a second time, when his eldest son already had a wife and child of his own, Farndale married his third wife, Eliza Sanford, with whom he had another son, David, in 2000. Three years later, Farndale Tech merged with another IT company led by Colin Mitchell, and the two men continued to run the business together until Farndale expressed a wish to retire and was bought out by Mitchell in 2007. Unable to live without a business project to turn his mind to, during his retirement Farndale oversaw the refurbishment and restructuring of the City Museum, which was renamed in his honour. Since being diagnosed with heart trouble in 2011, he had completely retired from public life, preferring to spend his remaining time with his family.

Even allowing for the fact that an obituary in the local paper was unlikely to be critical, Collins thought it looked as if Farndale had not been the kind of man who made enemies. His business dealings appeared to be all above board, and although he was married three times, there had been no acrimonious divorces. There was one very obvious reason why someone would have hurried him to the grave, though: an estate that was estimated at – give or take – twenty million pounds. It would be interesting to know how that was to be divided among his large family. He would get DS Holmes onto it.

Sally Holmes had been taken into care for the first time when she was three. She had returned home when her mother had kicked her habit, but it wasn't to be for long. When she was five social services took her away again, and when her mother died of an overdose, St Bride's Children's

Home became her permanent address. She never knew who her father was, and her grandparents, who had their only child late – and frankly, hadn't made a very good job of that one – were too old to take her in. She knew the other children at St Bride's dreamed about their parents, their *real* parents, coming to take them away. Some, like Matt Fielding, had never known them. Most had, and should have known better, in Sally's opinion. She did remember her mother, but she preferred not to. What she remembered was being unwanted, being inconvenient. It was easier to think of herself as not having parents, never having had them. It was only later that she learned that all children fantasise about their real parents being kinder and richer and more adventurous than the ones they really have. But Sally never had. She'd been all right at St Bride's. She had ups and downs, like any child, but nothing like some of the disturbed and mistreated children who were placed there temporarily when no foster family could be found. She'd taken what she was given, and had found her own way. St Bride's was in the past now, and all it had left her with was a less than rosy view of childhood and a dislike of stories with lovable orphans in them. She hadn't even read the Harry Potter books. Also, she hated it when people equated being in care with being maltreated or abused.

'That's so annoying,' she told Collins, 'And one of the reasons I don't talk about it, actually. When they hear you have been in care people always assume the worst. And that is so unfair to all those people who did and do their very best for the children they look after. And it's not as if being raised in a family protects you from abuse. I realised that even before I started my police training. The worst that ever happened during my time at St Bride's was a staff member who was stealing from the stores. The rest were all right.

I'm not in touch with any of the other children from that time now, but I still visit Miss Gardiner. She was the oldest and the most old-fashioned of the staff. She's in a home herself now.'

Matt had been a few years older than Sally, the only one left who had lived at St Bride's from a baby. She remembered him as a sort of dependable but distant older cousin. He had left to go to sixth-form college when she was thirteen, and she hadn't seen him since. Like her, he was not one of those who attended reunions and treated St Bride's like it was a big family. They had both been the kind who didn't really know what family was supposed to be.

She was glad Collins didn't make a big deal out of her story, or become oozily sympathetic. He just listened, and nodded, and returned to the matter in hand.

'So, you are acquainted with our witness who thinks he is a suspect.'

'Yes,' she said wearily, 'Is there a T-shirt I should buy?'

'No, you only do that once you fall in love with him.'

She snorted. 'Not guilty. All right, what do you want to know?'

'Well, what do you think of his story? From what you know of Matt Fielding, should we believe this tale?'

She considered this. 'I think it sounds very unlikely, but that's just it. Matt – how I remember him – he wouldn't make things up. I don't mean he *couldn't*, exactly, but when the younger kids – me included – went into hysterics about something he would always come up with the most simple explanation for what was upsetting us. We had these crazes, you know, like seeing ghosts, or believing there were giant rats living in the attic, whatever, and there he'd be, saying 'But isn't it more likely...' and you'd think, of course, we're being stupid. Well, that's what *I* would think, I think some of the others preferred the sensational versions. The thing is, the Matt I knew would only offer an outlandish explanation if he thought that was the most likely one. He wouldn't, well, fantasise.'

'You mean he wouldn't when he was a boy,' Collins said.

She shrugged her shoulders. 'Sure, people change, but being imaginative? I don't think that's a trait that changes much.'

'Could he have made it up as an elaborate cover?'

Sally had to think about that. 'Intellectually he would certainly be capable of it. But it does seem out of character. I'd expect, oh, I don't know, something less gothic, I suppose, something more straightforward.'

'Right,' the DI said, 'Well, I've called Dr Nakamura and the post-mortem is scheduled for tomorrow. With a bit of luck we'll know the cause of death, and then we can decide whether to pursue.'

Dr Nakamura rang them on Tuesday afternoon. Collins put the phone on speaker so Sally could listen in.

'I hear you are interested in a Mr Victor Farndale?'

'I am. His family are convinced he was murdered. What can you tell me?' Collins said.

'There is no question that he died a natural death,' she replied decidedly.

'So the family are wrong?' Sally asked hopefully.

'I didn't say that.'

'But—'

Dr Nakamura ignored the interruption. 'According to his records, Mr Farndale was on medication for a heart condition, and it was a heart attack which could have happened at any moment which killed him. There was something odd, though. I've sent blood and tissue for tests, and I'll be able to tell you more once I get the tox screen results. But for now, I can say that it is unlikely that Mr Farndale took his medication in the twenty-four hours prior to his death.'

'So it is possible someone prevented him taking them, intending it to be fatal?' Collins asked.

'Good luck arguing that in court. But yes, if you have other indications in that direction, it is certainly consistent with my findings. I'll be in touch once I know more about the chemical analysis.'

'Thank you, Dr Nakamura.'

Collins ended the call and they looked at each other.

'Matt was right, then,' Sally said at length.

'It seems we've got ourselves a case,' her colleague agreed.

5

'Is it always so untidy in here?' was the first thing Chief Inspector Dixon said when she came into his office for their 'getting to know each other' chat.

Collins looked around the room. There was the usual amount of paperwork on his desk. The suit he was supposed to take to the drycleaners was draped over a filing cabinet. His sports bag was lying in the corner, just in case he had time for the gym when he knocked off for the day. A stack of used cardboard coffee cups sat patiently on top of the printer, waiting to be recycled. The whiteboard he was supposed to use for cases was covered with a collage of photos and postcards. There were sticky notes on most vertical surfaces, not all of them pertinent. He suppressed the impulse to remove the nearest ones. This was his office, this was how he worked, and he wasn't going to pretend otherwise.

'Yes, it is. I'm good with chaos. Won't you sit down?'

They exchanged the usual basic information: where they were from, age, relationship status (Collins being extraordinarily pleased to have something to declare in that department), career in the police so far. Rowena was single and had joined the police through the graduate fast-track programme.

'I assume the same goes for you,' she said with a smile. She smiled a lot, the new DCI.

'No, in fact I took the standard route: Bramshill, three years in uniform, then a transfer to CID. I've been at this station my whole career, except for one year in Oxford.'

'Oxford! Then you know Addy Latimer?'

They chatted about the people they both knew there, and then Rowena said she'd better leave him to get on with things.

'How was it?' Sally asked, when he joined her in the CID room.

'Uninformative,' he said truthfully. 'But then you only get to know people by working with them, don't you?'

'I suppose so,' the sergeant said. She didn't sound convinced.

'Did you call Victor Farndale's solicitors?' he asked her.

'Yes, I did. They're Taylor, Weir & Taylor. At a rough estimate, after the deduction of estate tax and individual bequests, the children will each get around two million pounds. The bequests to the grandchildren are substantial, and – these are Mr Taylor's words, not mine – no one should have reason to feel hard done by.'

'So all of them are better off now than they were.'

'You can say that again.'

'Right, then I think it is time we paid a visit to Ulvercott House.'

'I'd no idea this was still a private residence,' Sally said as she drove them up to the house's imposing Palladian entrance front. But Collins had come prepared. There were certain advantages to moving in with someone else's library. Although most of the books were still in removal boxes, Dominic's book about notable houses in the county had been located in one of the upper strata, and it had told Collins that Ulvercott had started out as an abbey in the late middle ages, had become a private house after the dissolution, had briefly returned to being a religious retreat in the twentieth century, and was now in private hands again. Farndale had bought it in 1980, a few years after he married his second wife.

'Before Victor retired, the headquarters of Farndale Tech were in the west wing,' explained the neatly dressed white-haired lady who received them, 'But now they are in the new building in Abbey Hill. Do come through. I am Ursula Westmacott, Victor's sister-in-law. His first wife's sister, that is.'

She led the way through a hall with an impressive staircase. 'We were just having tea in the downstairs sitting room. You'll find most of the family are still here.'

They followed her into a large, south-facing room filled with people. Collins noticed that in contrast to its classical exterior, inside the house was furnished much like a suburban semi would be. It was clearly a home the family had been living in comfortably for decades, eclectic and a little shabby by now.

He introduced himself and DS Holmes, and explained why they had come.

'You took your time,' said a tall, grey-haired man in his forties.

This was not usually the reaction he got when coming to tell people they would be subject to a murder inquiry. 'I beg your pardon?'

'My father died on Saturday and you show up on Tuesday afternoon?'

Collins assumed that this was Victor's eldest son Robert, who had wanted to call the police at once. 'The post-mortem was conducted today, sir, and we are still awaiting further test results. I came here as soon as I received the pathologist's preliminary conclusions. Unfortunately it is not possible at this point to ascertain whether Mr Farndale died as the result of interference by person or persons unknown. We're treating his death as unexplained.'

'Nonsense, of course he was murdered,' Robert Farndale said brusquely.

'As I said, we are not in a position to say. But we are aware that concerns have been raised, and we are here to establish the sequence of events which led to your father's death.'

He didn't mention that he had already spoken to Matt Fielding. If the man was right – and it still seemed farfetched to him – his fiancée and her siblings were trying to point the finger at him to divert suspicion from one of themselves. He would wait and see how that played out.

While Sally explained that they wanted to talk to everyone who had been at Ulvercott House on Friday and Saturday, he mentally tried to match the faces in the room before him to the list of family and guests Fielding had provided. Ms Westmacott had introduced herself, and he had already identified Robert. One of the middle-aged women must be Victor's wife, and the handsome Asian woman must be the Ms Mahajan on his list. There was sufficient resemblance between the twenty-something man and the teenage boy to identify them as Farndale's sons from his second and third marriages respectively, and their twin sisters were also easy to pick out. But that still left a few question marks. He recognised Eden Kingston, the black girl, because he had met her before, but he had no idea what she was doing here, and there were two other young women he could not identify. He hadn't expected such a large gathering, but it might not be a bad thing. It saved having to explain the situation to each of them individually, at least.

'May I ask what led you to consider Victor's death as suspicious?' Ms Westmacott said, in a more conciliatory tone than Robert had used.

He saw no harm in telling her. 'I must stress that there is room for interpretation in the pathologist's conclusions, but we believe it possible that someone tampered with Mr Farndale's medication. If he had taken his daily dose the pathologist should have found traces in his system, but so far she has not.'

'Well, we had worked that much out for ourselves,' one of the young women said, sounding as impatient as her elder brother.

'May I ask how, Ms...?'

'Antigone Farndale. And we know because the scenario had been proposed before he died, by dad himself. It was the last time we were all together, over Christmas. He dined downstairs with us for once and Eliza brought him his pills. He took them and said something like 'without these I would be dead within two days'. Of course the younger ones where ghoulish enough to ask what would happen, and he explained about his heart condition and what the blood thinners were for. 'If you substituted these with a placebo my heart would have to work so hard that it would kill me by trying to keep going,' is what he said. And I suppose someone took note.'

'I see. And who was there at the time?'

Antigone sniffed. 'That's not going to help you much. Everyone who was here this weekend except Poppy, and I am sure Oliver told her – didn't you, Olly? Ironic, isn't it? Dad telling his own murderer how to do it.'

'It is certainly interesting, Ms Farndale. But I have to remind you that at present we cannot be sure that that is what happened. Now, if those of you who are not staying in the house would let DS Holmes know your addresses, we can make an appointment to talk to you. Anyone resident we will see here over the next few days. Is there a room the sergeant and I can use where we aren't too much in your way?'

'Jacqueline?' Ms Westmacott said.

'The old study, I think. No one uses it much,' the woman called Jacqueline replied. 'If we are finished here I will show you, Inspector. There's a broadband connection, if you need that.'

'Yes, that sounds perfect. Oh, and a SOCO team will be arriving sometime this afternoon to examine what may be the crime scene. I understand Mr Farndale's room has been left untouched since Saturday?'

'I locked his rooms myself,' Robert assured them.

'Good.'

As they left the downstairs sitting room, the Asian woman – he hadn't worked out yet how she was connected to the family – followed and held him back.

'It wasn't as dramatic as Antigone paints it, you know. When you come to talk to us all you will soon learn that Annabel's daughters have quite a flair for the theatrical,' she told him, 'Victor did say that about not surviving for two days without his tablets, and something about them looking just like other pills, but he didn't actually propose substituting them as a murder method. That is just how it sounds to us now he has died so suddenly.'

'But Mr Farndale's words could still have given someone the idea.'

'Clearly. I remember talking to Nora about it when we got home. The others probably did the same.'

Ah, Nora was the eldest daughter, so Ms Mahajan must be her partner. He thanked her for her information, and said he would talk to her later.

'I should introduce myself,' the woman called Jacqueline said as she shooed a cat out of the room they were to use. 'My name is Jacqueline Whyatt. I came to work here on a live-in basis after my divorce in 1992.'

That sounded familiar. 'Whyatt? Are you the Jacqueline Moss whose parents used to run the chippy in Abbey Hill?'

She looked at him blankly. 'Is Big Brother watching me? It seems the police really do know everything. But yes, that's me. I kept my husband's name after we separated, I never much liked Moss.'

'Sorry, not relevant, I know. But I spent some time investigating in Abbey Hill last year, and got to know the place pretty well.'

'Yes, the boy who disappeared,' she said, more animated now, 'I read that that case had been solved.'

'And what is your role at Ulvercott, Mrs Whyatt?'

'I'm the housekeeper. An old-fashioned term, that, but it is the one that best describes what I'm doing here. I look after the house, make sure the guest rooms are ready, keep the larder stocked, make arrangements for maintenance and repairs and so on. There's a daily woman who comes to do the cleaning, and sometimes, like last weekend, when there are a lot of guests, we hire extra help – Eden Kingston, in this case. If there is anything of a practical nature you need while you are in the house, you can ask me.'

'Thank you, Mrs Whyatt. We'll also need to talk to you later about Saturday's events. For now, could you show me where Mr Farndale's room is?'

'Of course.'

They left DS Holmes to arrange the study as an incident-cum-interview room, and moved across the landing.

'Since he became unwell Mr Farndale mostly kept to his own apartments,' Mrs Whyatt explained. 'There's a sitting room, a bedroom, and a dressing room with an en suite, with a single door into the passage.' She nodded in the direction of the door in question. 'Do you want to have a look?'

He shook his head. 'No, I'd better leave that to my colleagues from forensics. And Mrs Farndale's bedroom? I understood she was nearby when Mr Farndale had his attack.'

'The next one along, but there is no connecting door. David's room is further down the passage, and the rest of the family are all on the second floor.'

He returned to the study to find that Sally had arranged a desk with a laptop computer and a chair facing it for their interviewees.

'I've commandeered the room next door as well, so we can both talk to people at the same time.' She looked around the study, into which you could have fitted four standard interview rooms. 'What *did* people use all these rooms for?'

'Never mind that, what do you think about the case?'

She made a face. 'I'm thinking that I'd quite like to kick something. Or someone. We have – what? – sixteen people who benefit, and all of them heard the victim himself suggest a way to kill him.'

'At least it explains why they all jumped to the conclusion that he was murdered. I did wonder about that.'

'Let's hope they are not all in it together. Who are we seeing first?'

'Ms Westmacott, I think. If Mrs Whyatt is the old-fashioned housekeeper, she is surely the lady of the house.'

Ursula Westmacott, when she arrived, confirmed this idea.

'I came to live here – not at Ulvercott House, that is, but with Victor – when my sister died, to look after her children, and I never left,' she explained.

'Was that an informal arrangement or a paid position?' Sally asked.

'Informal. I did have a job at the time, I worked as copy-editor for Foley & Fletcher, the publishers. They would send me proofs, I corrected them and sent them back. Working from home is not exactly new in that sector. And it was work that was easy to combine with family life.'

'So you got to read the bestsellers before anyone else?'

'Once or twice. Although when you are engaged in spotting misplaced commas, you tend not to notice the story much. But that is not important at present. What do you want to know, Inspector?'

'First, I would like to know about Mr Farndale and his family. Just background, pretend I have never heard of Victor Farndale before. This is not a formal interview or an official statement, at present we're just gathering information.'

'Very well,' Ursula said, 'Victor.'

6

Ursula

Victor. Of everyone here at Ulvercott House I knew him longest. I won't say best. He was in many ways a very private man. I first met him in 1967 when he became engaged to my younger sister, Olivia. My parents did not take to him, and I tended to be on their side. He belonged to a different class, and he didn't try to pretend otherwise, he wasn't a man for compromises. Such things still mattered, more than they do now. Olivia was only twenty, and she had always had the best of everything. There was a selfish streak in her, too. Nothing conspicuous, she could be very considerate towards others. But what Olivia wanted, Olivia got, and she'd never known any different. She wanted Victor, and she married him, despite our parents' objections. And they were happy, I believe, although I did not see so much of them in those early years. They had very different personalities. Victor was always full of ideas, always exploring new opportunities, while my sister was conventional in many ways, even unimaginative. She was proud to have married an up-and-coming young man, and satisfied to live in a house that was beyond the means of her friends. But she was content with that, too. She didn't understand why Victor always wanted to move on to new things, to try daring schemes, to keep learning and meeting new people. She would have been perfectly happy to copy our parents' existence, and I think that had she lived, the marriage might have become very difficult as she settled and he kept moving. But we shall never know, because when she was twenty-seven Olivia died in a car accident. It was after her death that I moved in to look after her children. Robert and Nora were five and two years old, and naturally they had a difficult time. My moving in was supposed to be a temporary affair, until a nanny or something of the sort could be arranged, but it turned out to suit all of us, and I stayed on.

Victor married again in 1976. Robert was seven at the time, and resented Annabel's claims on his father's attention, but Nora didn't mind. She was always a stoic little thing.

Annabel Rokeby was an actress, a complete contrast to Olivia, and very focused on her career. It wasn't until 1985 that the twins were born. An au pair girl from Spain was engaged to help take care of them. I was never as involved in Electra and Antigone's upbringing as I was with my own nephew and niece, but this was a time when there were always guests staying at Ulvercott, and I often played hostess when Annabel was away at the theatre. Victor enjoyed having a house full of people, the more the merrier.

Maite, the Spanish girl, left after about a year, and I was sorry to see her go, she was very good with the little ones. We didn't get a replacement, though, because Annabel said she wanted to spend more time at home with her children. She probably believed this to be true, but it was also a way of not having to face that she was no longer being asked for the parts she wanted. It made her short-tempered and depressed, and she took prescription drugs in amounts I thought frankly unwise. She cut back while she was pregnant with Mortimer, but once he was born she returned to her old habits. She also returned to the stage, and for a while everything seemed fine. Farndale Tech was doing well, Robert and Nora were becoming independent, I was beginning to think that it was time I left the family and lived on my own again. And then, when Mortimer was ten and the twins thirteen, Annabel died of an accidental overdose.

Victor was devastated. It was the second time he lost a wife he loved, and he had been with Annabel for much longer than with Olivia. He threw himself into his work, and left the running of the house to me. There was no question of leaving now. Victor and I had long ago learned to get along, and I wanted to do everything I could to help. I was the one who saw that his children were clothed and fed, and who dealt with their schools and sports and so on.

Perhaps I should explain about the children's education. Olivia would have expected it, of course, and Victor wanted the best for his children, so Robert and Nora went to boarding school. But Annabel wouldn't hear about sending her children away, even though she was hardly ever at home herself, and the twins and Mortimer were in day schools. But when she died, Victor thought they would be better off at a boarding school than staying at home being reminded of their mother's absence. Electra and Antigone took to it, but I do not think Mortimer did. He was too young to understand that he hadn't been packed off for being a nuisance. He was never close to his father afterwards, and he prefers being with his friends to spending time with the family. Understandable, but I must say I do not think much of his friends.

So that's Victor's first and second family. You won't need me to tell you about his third, as you'll be speaking to them yourself. I wasn't at all sure it was a good idea for Victor to marry again, I thought we were quite happy and settled as we were, but it worked out very well, and David is a delightful boy. I'm afraid Victor's other children don't all think so. Robert was especially hostile when his father decided to take a new wife.

In 2011 Victor was diagnosed with heart trouble, and he has lived very quietly since. A qualified nurse – Ms Krupinska – came twice a week to check on him, and she put the right doses of his medication in the dispensing tray every Monday. Victor was careful about taking his pills, and in my opinion it is very unlikely that he would have forgotten them. He was a tidy, organised person, one of the few things we had in common.

There is one more thing I would like to add. Over the years a good many people have assumed that I was in love with my brother-in-law and that I resented his wives. That was never the case. It used to be common to suppose that a woman only remains single if she cannot get her man, and even nowadays very few people entertain the idea that I never married because when I was young it was not legally possible, but that was how it was. I am so glad things are different now for Nora and Sunita.

Victor Farndale could be an exasperating man and we disagreed about many things, but his family became my family, and I love his children and grandchildren as if they were my own.

7

On Wednesday morning, Collins took the floor in the CID meeting.

'We've got a possible murder case,' he told the team, 'Victor Farndale, seventy-two, died because he did not take, or was prevented from taking, his heart medication.'

'I have not seen a referral from the coroner for this,' DCI Dixon observed.

'It will probably arrive today, as soon as Dr Nakamura has submitted her report. But the family themselves had already raised concerns with us, and we've had SOCO at the scene, such as it was.'

'I did not authorise that,' the DCI interposed.

'No, ma'am. Is that a problem?'

Surely she did not expect him to run basic procedure by her for every new case?

'Just that I prefer protocol to be followed in all cases. But please continue.'

He explained the situation at Ulvercott House, and how the family thought Victor had been killed.

'That someone swapped the pills fits with Dr Nakamura's preliminary conclusions. The medication was not kept locked away, so everyone in the house had access.'

'Fingerprints?' DCI Dixon asked, clearly expecting SOCO to get on with it, authorised or not.

'The nurse's and Eliza's on the dispensing tray, as you'd expect, only Victor's own on the glass by his bedside.'

'And the cabinet where the pills were kept?'

'All of the above, plus Jacqueline Whyatt's.'

'I can't recall the last time fingerprints were actually useful in catching anyone,' DI Graham said, 'Not with a premeditated murder, anyway. Anything likely to yield DNA?'

'A single blond hair trapped in the hinges of the lid on the tray. We should be able to match that, but it wouldn't prove anything. Hair tends to get around. There's also a bit of fibre, wool, dark blue. We may be able to find the source of that, it may be from the gloves the perpetrator wore. But to start with this will be mostly establishing alibis, I think. DS Holmes and I will return to Ulvercott later to take statements.'

When DCI Dixon had left them to it, Collins turned to Peter Graham. 'What was that about? Do you ask for permission from the DCI before calling in SOCO?'

DI Graham shrugged. 'I didn't for the attack in Minster Street, but it was obvious there that a crime had been committed. I suppose we'd better stick to the letter of the law until we know where we stand with DCI Dixon.'

'It's always like that, isn't it?,' Sergeant Pardoe said sagely, 'If you authorise something off your own bat they say you're not following procedure, and when you follow procedure they tell you to show initiative and not to bother them with every little detail. She'll learn soon enough. Now, this murder of yours, you didn't say who benefits. You must have some idea.'

Sally rolled her eyes. 'The children and grandchildren. All of them. I've phoned Taylor, Weir & Taylor. Fifty thou each to his grandchildren and to Juliette Westmacott – that's the niece – to be held in trust for those who are not yet of age, and other substantial bequests to the elder Miss Westmacott and several non-profit organisations. The remainder of his estate is to be divided equally between his six children.'

'Doesn't his wife get anything?' DC Robbins asked, surprised.

Sally shook her head. 'At Mrs Farndale's own request, she is not named in her husband's will. I understand she wanted to avoid any suspicion that she had married her husband for financial gain.'

'That still leaves sixteen people with a motive,' Collins said, counting them on his list. 'So we'd better get on with it.'

Their first witness of the day was Katarzyna Krupinska, the private nurse who had looked after Mr Farndale. She was a Polish woman in her forties, with only the faintest trace of an accent.

'I am a qualified nurse, and I visit Mr Farndale two mornings a week, or more often when there is cause for concern.'

'Can you tell us about Mr Farndale's medication?'

'Mr Farndale's pills are kept in the cabinet in his dressing room. It is not locked. He took his twice daily dose of both kinds from one of those boxes with compartments for every day of the week. I put Mr Farndale's tablets in it every Monday. He never forgot, but his wife or Jacqueline would check daily if he had taken them just to be sure.'

'At what time of day did he take his medicine?'

'Just after breakfast and just after dinner. He had a routine, and he stuck to it.'

'And everyone in the household was familiar with this routine?'

'I assume so. Of course I wasn't actually in the house most of the time, but I spoke to Mrs Farndale and Jacqueline about how Mr Farndale was doing.'

'And how had he been doing recently?'

She smiled faintly. 'As well as could be expected. You must understand that his prognosis wasn't good, all we could do was manage his condition. He was not in pain, but he tired very easily. It could be very frustrating for him – I understand he used to be a very active kind of man.'

'And there was no change in the last week or so?'

She thought for a moment. 'He seemed agitated on one of my visits. I asked him if something had happened to worry him, but he was evasive. He said 'it could be good news, in a way, we'll see', and that is all I could get out of him.'

'Can you recall when this was, exactly?'

'It was on the Monday. I remember I was dispensing his pills at the time.'

'I see. And you noticed nothing unusual about the pills?'

'Is that what they think happened, then? Someone tampered with his pills?'

'Do you think it is possible?'

She shook her head. 'Not with the stock in the cabinet. They come in blister packs. If someone messed with them it must have been later, when they were already in the dispensing tray.'

When the nurse had gone, Collins turned to Sally. 'Does she get anything in Farndale's will?'

DS Holmes looked at her notes. 'No, nothing. She clearly had the opportunity – she visited on Friday morning – but she's about the only one without a motive.'

'Without a *financial* motive,' Collins amended, 'And she's not the only one in that situation. Let's go and talk to the widow.'

8

Eliza

Of course most people thought I married Victor for his money. That's why I insisted that he leave me nothing substantial in his will. I think it satisfied the children that my motives were not mercenary, but of course it is nonsense to say that I get nothing. During our time together Victor paid all the bills. I have worked for fifteen years without spending a penny of my own salary on necessities. My son's education will be paid out of his own inheritance. I may not be what Robert and his wife would call rich, but believe me, I am well provided for.

Victor was fifty-seven when we married, and I was thirty-nine. Robert always made out I was some seductive siren taking advantage of a man in his dotage – which was insulting to his father as well as to me. It didn't help that I was his secretary, of course. Well, management assistant, but in other people's mouths it always became 'secretary'. I had been working for him for five or six years by then. My last relationship had ended badly, and I wasn't looking for passion, I was looking for someone steady to have a child with. Insofar as I had an ulterior motive in marrying, that was it: I was nearing forty and I wanted a child. I wasn't in love with Victor, but we got along, we knew we worked well together, and I could see he was a good father to his other children, I didn't have to think for long when he proposed. We were married in '99 and David was born a year later.

I have never regretted my decision, and I am grateful for the time I had with Victor, but in the early years it wasn't easy. As I said, Robert and Nora behaved as if I were a young gold-digger taking advantage of a silly old man, and it must have been strange for them, me being closer in age to them than to him, and Robert himself already married. But Victor wasn't sixty yet, and there has never been anything silly about him. Nora came round when David was born, she adores him, but I think Robert still hasn't got used to me. It was different with the twins and Mortimer. Electra and Antigone had lost their mother, and there was never any question of my taking on that role. They were away at boarding school most of the time, and when they were here Ursula looked after them. They treated me in the same way they did Jacqueline, as someone who just happened to be there, nothing to do with them. I did try to be more motherly for Mortimer, but he has always been the most reserved of Victor's children, so I have no idea how much of that got through. We get along fine, to all intents and purposes, but I can never tell what he is thinking.

All Victor's older children are more like aunts and uncles to David than siblings, and when he became ill my husband was more a grandfather than a father to his child. But David is a happy boy, I think we both gave him the best we could give.

I knew my husband was ill, and although seventy-two is no great age these days, I was aware he might not have long. But this is so sudden— I keep expecting Victor to call me upstairs because there is some new idea he wants to talk about. He never lost his interest in business developments, you know, or his enthusiasm for the inventions of others. He was disappointed, I think, that none of his children showed much entrepreneurial spirit. They all take after their mothers, in that respect. Of course I never met my predecessors, but I know Victor married three very different women, and you can see that in his children. I sometimes think that by the time I came along, Robert had still not recovered from the shock of Annabel. I once asked him if he and Bettina had named Bella after her, and you should have seen the look on his face. He couldn't tell me fast enough that Bettina's mother was called Isabella. He's so unimaginative, Robert, he must get that from his mum. Certainly not from Victor, and it's a complete contrast to the twins. In a funny way I wish I'd known Annabel. From what Ursula has told me she sounds a remarkable woman.

I have no idea who could have killed my husband. The obvious motive is money, I suppose, but although I know my stepchildren to be capable of unkindness, I find it hard to imagine them capable of murder. And I cannot think of any other reason why someone would want Victor dead. There may easily be something in his past I do not know about, of course. He lived a whole life before I even met him. And there was something... I wouldn't say he was upset, last week, more like he was excited by something, excited and troubled at the same time. I'm sure he would have told me about it eventually, but he didn't have the time.

9

Eliza Farndale pressed her handkerchief to her eyes. 'That's all I can tell you.'

'Thank you, that will do for now,' Collins told her, 'We would like to talk to your son as well. In your presence, of course.'

Eliza took a deep breath. 'I think, perhaps... Could you ask Ursula, if she doesn't mind? I mean, David's fourteen, I'm sure you'd rather talk to him without his mum present.'

She was right about that, but Sally thought her real reason was probably that she would break down if she had to talk about her husband any more. She had the impression of a woman barely holding it together. Eliza might not have been in love when she married Victor, but she obviously cared a lot.

She found Ursula Westmacott in the garden and asked her to come to the incident room while Owen hunted down David.

Like his mother, David was both matter of fact about his father's death and visibly upset by it. They asked him what it was like to have a father old enough to be your grandfather.

'Sometimes I didn't like it. He couldn't come to the football like other fathers. I don't mean because he was old – some of the other guys have grandparents who come and watch – but because he was ill. He was tired all the time, and he had five other children who also wanted his attention.'

'Do you get along with your brothers and sisters?'

'Not all of them. Robert is the worst. I think he really resented mum marrying dad. Nora is okay, she's just like an aunt, really. And Robert could have been a kind of uncle if he had wanted, but he barely speaks to me. Which is really stupid, when you think about it. Dad wasn't exactly pleased at his reaction, so then Robert saw even less of him than the rest of us. I bet when you talk to him Robert will go on about what a bad father Victor was. But that's just not true.'

'And what about Mortimer and your sisters?'

David shrugged. 'Mortimer's all right. But he's a very private person, I don't see much of him even though we live in the same house.'

'And the twins?'

David smiled for the first time, for a moment looking just like his mother. 'They're the opposite of private, they always want to talk. Sometimes it feels like they are the teenagers here even though they are, like, twice my age.'

Sally caught an amused look, quickly suppressed, on Ursula Westmacott's face. She was beginning to be very curious about Electra and Antigone. But the twins would have to wait.

'I think it's time we spoke to Robert Farndale,' Collins said, when David had gone.

'I'm sure so does he. Shall I call him in?'

'Let me be frank, Inspector,' Robert Farndale said, before pausing portentously. Collins always wondered why people bothered saying that. Surely it implied that being frank was the exception rather than the rule? It just made them regard what came next with suspicion.

'I did not always approve of my father's actions, especially in regard of how he treated his family. Indulgent one time, neglectful the next. As for this third marriage, at his age it was simply irresponsible.'

'He was fifty-seven, I believe?'

'Exactly. Preposterous.'

Robert Farndale was forty-six now. Collins wondered if he'd still find the idea preposterous in ten years' time.

'Both my children are older than my youngest brother. It was time for my father to be their grandfather, but no, he had to indulge himself and take another wife.' He shook his head. 'She married him for the money, of course.'

'And you think she killed him for it?'

'That's going a bit far!'

'You have made no secret of the fact that you believe your father was murdered. Presumably you have some theory as to by whom,' Collins insisted.

'Well obviously, if he was murdered, someone from Ulvercott must have done it. Someone with access to the house, I mean. But I just cannot believe any member of the family would do such a thing.'

That was coming perilously close to saying the servants must have done it, Collins thought. 'Who else had access to the house? Specifically, who was here on Friday or Saturday?'

Mr Farndale made a show of pondering this. 'There's the nurse, of course, that Eastern European woman. Mr Taylor – the solicitor – came to see my father on Friday morning. And there was a vicar who paid a visit, Jacqueline said. Very odd, that, my father was not religious.'

'There's a hypothesis for you,' Collins told Sally when Robert had left, 'Man of the cloth wanders in off the street and decides to convince an atheist of the existence of heaven by the direct route.'

'I suppose we'll have to check it out,' Sally said, making a note of it, 'Although he could have been visiting anyone in the house.'

'You're right, of course. We'll have to check the solicitor as well, but despite Mr Farndale's protestations, I'm inclined to think they kept it in the family in this case.'

'Probably,' she agreed, 'And I don't know about the rest of what he was saying – I just don't get families – but I know he is wrong about one thing.'

'And that is?'

'Eliza was telling the truth when she said she didn't marry Victor for his money.'

'How do you figure that out?'

'Three happy marriages, not a hint of adultery, even his sapphic sister-in-law hasn't got a bad word to say about him. Never mind the millions, there was a man who knew how to treat a woman. Eliza Sanford knew what was good for her. And there's the will, remember? She isn't the one who gets her hands on the dough.'

What she said made sense, Collins thought.

'While Robert Farndale stands to inherit a pretty penny. Maybe you should go back to the station, check Robert's background. Especially his finances.'

'Right. But don't you want to speak to the others together as well?'

He looked down at his list, which had grown considerably since the morning meeting. 'No, we might as well split them between us, or we'll be ages. I'll talk to Robert's wife now, and you can have his twin sisters tomorrow.'

Compared to her husband, Bettina McKinley was a relief, simply because she wasn't so antagonistic. She took the chair opposite him, crossed her legs, tucked a strand of blonde hair behind her ear, and assured him she would do anything to help. Apparently, she and Robert had decided to stay on at Ulvercott House for the time being, rather than returning to their country house or their London flat.

'You did not need to return to work?' Collins asked her.

'I'm a freelance writer, so I don't have to turn up at the office. I write on interior decoration, women's magazines, mostly. You won't have heard of me. That is, I assume you are not a reader of *Good Housekeeping* or *Country Homes & Interiors*.'

He nodded. The only magazine – if that was the right word – he'd recently leafed through was a copy of *Medium Aevum* which Dominic appeared to have purloined from the uni library.

He asked Bettina about her father-in-law.

'I liked Victor. He has always made us very welcome here, and he was just the same with Poppy on Saturday.'

'Poppy is your son's girlfriend?'

'Fiancée. Victor was pleased with the engagement, he was always happy with a new addition to his family.'

Collins could feel a 'but' hanging in the air and didn't say anything.

'He could have been more supportive of the children, though. I mean my husband's younger siblings, and Oliver and Bella. Victor had some theory that it was good for their character if they had to make their own way in the world. He would pay for their education, but they had to get a job, and if they wanted to go on living here they had to pay for their board and lodging. I ask you! And all the while they knew that his money was waiting for them. Naturally it made them rather resent the policy.'

Collins didn't think this was natural at all. Surely expecting one's children to make their own way was reasonable from a parent, let alone a grandparent. And what if Victor had lived into his nineties? Were they supposed just to sit around waiting for entitlement to land in their laps like a bunch of provincial Princes of Wales? But it was interesting that Bettina clearly disagreed with Victor's views. There had been no such signs of tension when they had spoken to Ursula and Eliza.

When he had finished talking to Bettina, Collins decided to take a stroll around the garden before going home, to take in the lie of the land.

Ulvercott Park, which had once belonged to the house, was now a municipal green space with a mountain bike trail and other sports facilities, and only the gardens behind the house – still substantial – now belonged to the Farndales. At some point the entrance to the property had been moved to Newbury Road, the main road out of town. What had once been the lodge was now a tea room overlooking the drive. There was a bus stop just outside the gate.

The garden behind the house was well-kept, but rather soulless. He didn't think any of the Farndales were enthusiastic gardeners, and the place was probably still kept up by the firm who had looked after it when Ulvercott was Farndale Tech's main office. It had that corporate look about it, picknick tables included. There was a small pond in an ersatz Japanese garden which, disconcertingly, had several dead fish floating in it. Had someone forgotten to feed them since Victor's death? Did fish in garden ponds even need feeding?

If he started to speculate about the care and feeding of ornamental fish, it was probably time to go home.

As Sally drove back to her flat in Rivergate, she thought about the Farndale family, and the way they all seemed to accept as a matter of course that a murder had been committed – probably by one of their own. Matt Fielding's idea that someone wanted to frame him seemed less fantastical now she had seen the set-up at Ulvercott House. She supposed that Robert Farndale was the obvious suspect, especially now she had seen the state of his finances. He wasn't quite about to go under, but he definitely had cash flow problems. On the other hand, given the amounts circulating in the property business, Robert's inheritance probably wouldn't make much of a difference. Sally found it very hard to imagine a situation in which two million pounds was *not enough money*, but she supposed the Farndales were used to thinking in that order of magnitude. How on earth had Matt Fielding got himself mixed up with all that?

She had not seen Matt while they were at the house. Of course not, he would have been at work, unlike the likes of Robert Farndale, who could afford to hang around. She should be glad that she hadn't seen him, really, it looked like this case was going to be complicated enough without her own memories getting in the way, but instead Sally was vaguely disappointed. She would have liked to have a chat with Matt, hear how the years in between had treated him. I'm just curious, she told herself, and that's a good quality in a detective. Just curious, no more than that.

10

The first person Collins saw at Ulvercott House the next morning was Nora Farndale, Victor's eldest daughter. She came into the incident room with some sheets of paper in her hand.

'I needed something to do, so I typed up a chronology of events for you, Inspector. Only accurate from when we arrived at Friday noon, I'm afraid, but otherwise I think it gives a good overview.'

'Thank you, Ms Farndale, that is very helpful.'

She nodded in a businesslike manner. 'I would like to help, but I'm not good at all this talking about feelings stuff. The girls – Electra and Antigone, I mean – have all sorts of wild theories, but I simply can't imagine why anyone would want to kill Victor. Are you quite certain it was deliberate?'

'We are certain that your father did not take the right pills on the day he died. And yes, we suspect he was deliberately prevented from taking them.'

'I see,' she said, 'Still, I did not think it so very unlikely that Victor had died a natural death. He did have a heart condition, after all. And the way he had been talking to us in the past few months... as if he knew he didn't have long. And I could have done without Robert blustering and the twins throwing accusations around.'

'So you do not have any theories yourself?'

'None, Inspector. Shall I ask Sunita to come and speak to you now?'

Sunita Mahajan came straight from outside, and was still divesting herself of her coat when she came into the incident room. He couldn't help noticing that she wore dark blue gloves. Of course, in this weather it would have been more remarkable if she hadn't worn any gloves at all, the temperature was near to freezing. Perhaps that was what had done for the fish?

Ms Mahajan sat down, and told her story without any prompting from Collins. 'Nora and I met at teacher training college – she's Science, I'm English – and we've been together ever since. I first came here when Annabel was still alive. I recall the house always being full of people. Business associates of Victor's from America just loved being put up in a stately home, and Annabel always had people from her latest production over at all hours. Then there were Ursula and Jacqueline, and after her parents divorced, Juliette would come to stay in the holidays. That was how Victor loved it, everybody was welcome.'

She smiled reminiscently. 'Nora is always very down to earth, and I think she was a bit embarrassed with her family in a way. I suppose they could be tiresome at times, but to me they were a blessing. They were used to all sorts staying here – the addition of a lesbian Hindu to the household barely caused a ripple.'

'And that was a relief?'

'Not quite in the way you mean. I'm the youngest of five, and third generation English. By the time I got to my teens, most of the battles had been fought. I reckoned that if I just went my own way without making a song and dance about it, I'd be fine. I've been right about that, on the whole. Although there was one very awkward conversation with my mother about there not going to be any more grandchildren.'

'You and Nora never wanted children?'

'No, we did the opposite to her father. He was an orphan and always wanted a family. We both grew up in big families and decided not to have one of our own.'

'And you got on well with Mr Farndale?'

'Yes, Victor never treated me any different than he did Bettina, it wouldn't have occurred to him.'

'He sounds like a good man.'

'He was that. Although he was not always easy to get along with. Autocratic is the right word, I think. And he never said anything just to be nice. That could be hard on the younger ones especially – Olly and Bella and David. That generation is used to being coached through everything, and praised whenever they get something right. Victor's idea of praise was 'I haven't found anything wrong with it yet'. That makes him sound unpleasant, which he wasn't, really. But he could be very annoying for people who disagreed with him, because he simply wouldn't take other people's opinions into account. He never tried to talk people around to his point of view, if you disagreed you were just expected to lump it. And we did, because even if you thought he was being wrong-headed, you always knew he was being wrong-headed in what he thought was a good cause. At least, *we* all knew that. I cannot speak for his employees.'

'Do you know of any serious disagreements?'

'The kind that lead to murder? Not really. But then I can't really imagine what would. Robert and Victor rarely saw eye to eye, and I know Victor disapproved of the way Robert ran his own business. But I don't think anything explosive had happened recently. They had some flaming rows when Victor married Eliza, I wouldn't have been surprised by murder then. But lately we have all rubbed along quite happily.'

While Sally talked to Electra Farndale she couldn't help trying to see what had attracted Matt Fielding to her. He had always been a no-nonsense kind of guy, and from what she had seen on Monday he still was. Electra couldn't, by any stretch of the imagination, be described as a no-nonsense kind of woman. She wasn't exactly pretty, but she was skilfully made up, and one visit to a hairdresser for her probably covered Sally's budget for an entire year. She wore the kind of tailored clothes that were as far removed from high street fashion as it was possible to get without wearing a twinset and pearls. Everything about her screamed wealth and privilege, and Sally had to work very hard to keep her instant dislike in check.

She led with a few innocent questions about Electra's background.

'I do PR at the City Theatre. Part-time.'

'And you still live at home?' Sally asked, trying not to make this sound accusing. The woman must be nearly thirty.

'It's better than some poky flat. Tig and I did that when we were in London.' She shuddered theatrically. 'This beats anything we could afford for ourselves.'

'So that means you were familiar with your father's routine.'

'We all were. Although I must say I hadn't expected anyone to—' Electra took a shaky breath and dropped her voice '—*murder him*. Although I suppose it is always a danger, when someone is elderly and very rich.'

'It is also an enormous risk,' Sally said.

Electra considered this. 'Maybe not. It's not unusual for people to wander into dad's rooms to say hello or borrow a book or something. There's no one I would have been surprised to see coming out of there.'

Sally asked her if she suspected anyone in particular.

'Well, I hate to say it, but... Tig's boyfriend? You know what happened with his family, of course, you probably were on the case.'

Sally nodded. She had been, when she was still a DC. She thought she could see where this was heading.

'Well, I do wonder if he's quite... stable, you know what I mean? After all that. Perhaps murdering dad isn't as strange to him as it is for other people.'

'And why do you think he'd do that?'

She shrugged. 'Tig and I are both going to be rich now. He probably wanted a share.'

The money again. Could it really be so prosaic? Sally thanked Electra for her time and asked her to send in her sister.

Antigone and Electra were not identical twins, but they were still very alike. Their voices were nearly the same, and they had the same mannerisms. They also had the same tendency to plumpness, but apparently Antigone was better at dieting, because she was wearing a little black dress her sister would certainly not have been able to squeeze into. Two minutes into her conversation with Antigone, Sally had decided she understood Matt's preference for Electra after all, if her twin was the alternative. Antigone couldn't mention anyone, family or outsider, without throwing in a disparaging remark or two.

'I'd say that Eliza had got tired of waiting, that would make the most sense,' was her opening gambit, 'But she doesn't actually get a penny in dad's will. Of course David gets as much as any of us, so that could be your motive. But I'd call it unlikely.'

Then why bring it up? Sally wondered. She didn't say anything, though. It was best just to let a mouthy witness carry on, they always let on more than they knew themselves.

11

Antigone

Electra and I both live here. I know it's a bit lame, still living in your parents' house at our age, but who wouldn't prefer Ulvercott to some dreary little flat in town? It's cheaper, too. The gallery doesn't pay that well. Oh, perhaps I should have started with that. I work for the art gallery on Charter Street. It is where I met Simon, my boyfriend, who is an art historian. He writes our catalogue descriptions. Simon and I have been together since last summer, and he has visited Ulvercott several times, he gets along well with the rest of my family.

I picked up Simon after I finished work on Friday and we drove to Ulvercott. All the family were here, and it was a lovely weekend right up to Saturday evening. It was about eight, I think, when Eliza called Robert upstairs. He came back a minute later to say that she had found dad unresponsive and an ambulance was on its way. They took dad to the hospital, but it was too late by then.

Do I have to talk about this? It brings it all back, you see, the time when my mother died. The ambulance, the waiting, and then the bad news. She was such a wonderful woman, and we had so little time with her. Of course I know this is different. With his heart, we were lucky to have dad still with us all this time. I know I should be grateful, really. And I think killing dad was an ungrateful thing to do. Everyone who benefits from his death needed only to wait, we all knew he was unlikely to live very long. I suppose that means it can't be anyone who was really close to him. Apart from that we all loved him, no one is in financial difficulties, and we all would have inherited eventually. It has to be someone who didn't know that it was only a matter of time, someone who needs the money now and didn't know dad would have died soon anyway. I didn't tell Simon how bad it really was, and I'm sure Electra didn't tell Matt, but after dad's little performance at Christmas, we didn't need to, did we?

I'd hate to think it of Matt, but what if he was only using Electra to get close to Victor? We are well off, and that attracts some dubious types, we are all used to that. I expect soon enough there will be hopeful girls hanging around David. Anyway, if it is about money, I'd bet on Matt Fielding. Or Juliette, I suppose, she's always been jealous of what we have. But I do think she loved dad in her way, I can't imagine her wanting to murder him.

Nor can I imagine my brothers doing anything like this. Robert is much too strait-laced. And Mortimer... Well, okay, he is a bit weird. He never goes out like a normal person, all he does is play that football simulation game with his friends. It isn't healthy, if you ask me. He must have an addictive personality, like mum. But like her, he wouldn't hurt a fly. That's what they say, isn't it? Actually, Mortimer probably could hurt someone if he was angry enough. But not murder. I mean, I know I'm probably biased, we're talking about my little brother here, but I don't think he'd have the nerve. Can you imagine making the substitution and then just having to act normally for a day or more, waiting for something to happen? I can't see Mortimer doing that.

12

After Sunita Mahajan had left, Sally came in from the anteroom, and they compared notes.

'Robert's antagonism seems to be a theme,' Collins said.

'Yes, but there's nothing concrete. I've got one interesting titbit for you, though. This Simon who is in a relationship with Antigone, look.'

She showed him the contact details Antigone had given her.

'You can't be serious. Antigone's boyfriend is Simon Danvers?'

'It was all I could do to keep my face straight. They are like bad pennies, aren't they? The Danvers family.'

It was funny in a way, but— 'I had hoped to keep Jake out of an investigation for once.'

Collins had befriended Simon's brother Jake – at the time still a drug-pushing rent-boy – on a case three years ago. Since then the young man had been through some pretty severe ups and downs, mainly because first his family and then his fellow students had been involved in criminal cases.

'Cheer up,' Sally said, 'With a bit of luck Electra and Antigone are just fantasising about each other's boyfriends being involved. I get the impression they do that a lot, fantasising.'

'That's a good point Antigone makes though, about the murderer having to hold their nerve, waiting for things to happen.'

'Yes, it is. Can you see any of them doing that?' she asked.

'Ursula, I'd say, and perhaps Nora. She's very calm.'

'Anyway, whoever it was was good at it, because no one was acting strange, they all agree that nothing odd happened on Saturday. Only Victor himself had been troubled by something, according to his wife and Ms Krupinska.'

'Hm, yes, we really have to find out what that was about. Have you noticed that none of the others refers to that? A bit strange, don't you think? This whole household revolved around Victor, you'd think someone would have noticed.'

'I'm not sure about that,' Sally said, 'I get the impression most of the Farndales believe that the world revolves around themselves.'

'Possibly. Or possibly they do not want us to know what Victor was so agitated about.'

In the afternoon, Sally drove to the Priory Heights campus to talk to Robert and Bettina's son Oliver, who was a business management student there. When Sally was a student they had better things to do on weekends than attend dull family gatherings, but apparently Oliver had been at Ulvercott House from Friday afternoon through Sunday, with his girlfriend Poppy arriving on Saturday.

'Juliette – Ursula's niece – had already arrived before we did,' he told her, 'And the girl who was helping Jacqueline, Eden. I don't know her last name. She was there on Friday and Saturday afternoon. I liked her. My family can be pretty depressing at times, you know. It was nice to have someone cheerful around.'

'Depressing in what way?' Sally asked, dismissing the idea that the presence of the hired help was significant.

Oliver smiled wryly in a way that made him look older than his years. 'It's like when they go back to Ulvercott they also go back to being Victor's children, instead of being proper adults. The way dad goes on about being the eldest son, it's embarrassing, frankly.'

He smiled again, disarmingly this time, but Sally didn't smile back. As far as she was concerned, no one with a complete set of healthy, non-abusive parents had much reason to complain.

'Still,' Oliver continued, 'This weekend was better than most. I introduced Poppy to grandfather, and Matt and Simon were there, so it wasn't all Farndales.'

'Can you tell me who was in the house on Friday and Saturday?'

He did so, and Sally looked at the timeline Nora had made to see if it tallied with what Oliver told her. There had been a lot of coming and going on Friday afternoon and Saturday, and it was hard to tell if there was anyone who *didn't* have the opportunity to slip into Victor's rooms at some point.

While Sally was at the university, Collins talked to Jacqueline Whyatt in the kitchen of Ulvercott. As soon as he sat down, a long-legged black cat jumped onto the chair beside his and sniffed his hand.

'That's Foundling, he's very curious. You're not allergic, are you? I can put him outside.'

'No, please don't bother, I'm all right,' he said, as the cat rubbed its head against his sleeve. 'He's called Foundling?'

Collins wondered if that was insensitive, in the house of a man who had started life as one, or just a healthy sign that the past didn't haunt the Farndales.

'Yes, because we found him as a kitten, poor thing, not a sign of his mum or the rest of the litter. I suppose I'll have to find a home for him now.'

'Surely one of the family will want to keep the cat, even if they move?'

Jacqueline put a mug of tea in front of him. 'Oh, none of the family care much for pets, although I think David would like a dog. Foundling isn't anyone's, really. Anyway, that's hardly why you're here.' She sat down across from him. 'I expect you want to know about the family?'

He stroked Foundling's back, and just let her talk.

'I've been here since 1991, when Annabel was still alive. There has never been any question that I am just an employee, I certainly wouldn't call myself part of the family, and I have always tried to stay out of their little dramas. Or not so little, as the case might be. But it was different when Mr Farndale married Eliza. We are close together in age, and she was no more used to all this luxury than I was before coming here. We've become friends. And I feel for her now, with all those children making this into *their* tragedy, while nobody stops to think that she has just lost her husband.' She shook her head. 'They think she married him for his money, which is simply not true. Or because she wanted a child, which *is* true. But neither means that she didn't love him. I think she did, more than she expected to. She'll miss him.'

After asking her about her working relationship with her employer, which had been uneventful, Collins showed her Nora's timeline. 'Could you look at this and tell me if there is anything incorrect? Or if there is anything you wish to add?'

She leafed through it quickly. 'I think it is accurate, except that Bella was also here on the Friday. She came to pick up her field hockey things, she had a match on Saturday. But she only stayed long enough to fetch her bag from her room, and that's on the other side of the house from Mr Farndale's.

She said she wanted to catch the next bus, as she only had permission to be away from school for the afternoon. She goes to Overdene House.'

He made a note of this. 'That should be easy enough to check.'

A quick call with Bella's housemistress (housemistress! which century did they think they were in?) provided confirmation that she had been given permission to fetch her sports bag from her grandfather's house, and the unsolicited information that it was not at all like Bella to forget her things, she was usually very organised, which was why the lapse had been forgiven on this occasion. Collins thought uncharitably that it had probably more to do with not wanting to miss their star player for the match. Overdene House had won 5-1. After the match Bella had returned to Ulvercott for the family gathering as previously arranged, and despite her grandfather's sudden death she had been driven back to school by her father on Sunday evening, just as Nora had said. Someone would need to go there and talk to her.

13

Nora

Chronology of events of the weekend of 31 January, by Elinor (Nora) Farndale

FRIDAY

12:00
Sunita and I arrived, just in time to say hello to Eliza before she left for work. She told us that Victor had some visitors that morning, but I cannot tell you about anyone's movements before noon.

13:00
Present at lunch: Victor; Ursula; Electra; Nora; Sunita. Jacqueline was in the house but did not eat with us. Her assistant Eden also arrived around this time.

14:00
Ursula went out to meet a friend. Victor went to his room.

15:00
Sunita and I had coffee with Jacqueline in the kitchen. At around half past David came home from school.

16:00
Robert and Bettina arrived by car with Oliver. They went to see Victor in his room, Robert and Bettina joined us in the

front room afterwards, but I do not know where Oliver went. Electra came home from her job. Jacqueline's assistant Eden left, Ursula returned.

17:00
Juliette arrived on the bus, Antigone and Simon by car. They all went to see Victor in his room. I walked in the garden with Ursula. Eliza returned.

18:00
Present at dinner: Eliza; David; Nora; Sunita; Robert; Bettina; Oliver; Electra; Antigone; Simon; Juliette.
Mortimer came home from work and left again almost immediately, but I do not know where he went. Victor had dinner in his room.

19:00
David left for his shift at the supermarket. Electra's fiancé Matt arrived.

20:00
Ursula went to her book club.

22:00
Sunita and I went up to our room. Some time after this David and Ursula came back. Whether Mortimer returned to the house I do not know, I did not see him again until the next afternoon.

SATURDAY

08:00-10:00
People walked in and out of the kitchen to have breakfast.

10:00
Matt Fielding spent some time with Victor upstairs.

11:00
Sunita and I had coffee with Robert and Bettina in the downstairs drawing room. Electra and Antigone went into town with Juliette, Matt and Simon.

12:00
David was picked up by the father of one of his friends to take them to their football match.

13:00
Oliver's girlfriend Poppy arrived, at the same time as Eden. Robert left by car to pick up Bella from her school.

14:00
Oliver took Poppy up to meet Victor since it was her first time at the house.

15:00
The young people returned from town. I talked to Matt about science teaching.

16:00
Present at tea: Ursula; Bettina; Oliver; Poppy; Electra; Matt; Antigone; Simon; Juliette; Mortimer; Nora; Sunita.
At about a quarter to five Robert came back with Bella.

17:00
Eden left. Sunita and Juliette helped Jacqueline in the kitchen. David returned from playing football.

18:00
Present at dinner: Ursula; Robert; Bettina; Oliver; Poppy; Bella; Electra; Matt; Antigone; Simon; Juliette; Mortimer; Nora; Sunita.

19:00
Everyone went to their own rooms after clearing up the dinner things. We would normally have reconvened downstairs for a drink at nine.

20:00
Eliza heard a sound from Victor's room and found that he had collapsed. She called 999. Emergency services arrived and CPR was attempted. Eliza went with Victor in the ambulance.

21:00
At 21:40 Eliza rang Robert to say that Victor had been pronounced dead on arrival.

22:00
I drove to the hospital to pick up Eliza. When we got back to Ulvercott she told us that Victor's death would be referred to the coroner, and that there would probably be an autopsy.

23:00
We discussed the possibility that Victor was murdered. Robert decided to lock Victor's rooms in anticipation of a visit from the police.

SUNDAY

08:00-10:00
People walked in and out of the kitchen to have breakfast.

10:00
Ursula went to church.

11:00
We had coffee and the discussion about possible murder was resumed. Afterwards Eliza made phone calls to inform her friends and family about Victor's death. Robert called Victor's business associates to tell them the news.

13:00
Present at lunch: everyone.

14:00
After lunch Sunita and I decided to get out for a bit and went for a walk.

16:00
We returned to Ulvercott. By this time both Simon and Matt had left. Like Robert and Bettina, we decided that in the circumstances we had best stay on. Oliver and Poppy, who both had to be at their respective colleges on Monday, did return home.

19:00
Robert left to return Bella to her school.

NB: apart from Victor's unexpected death, there was nothing unusual about the weekend's events.

14

Before Collins could call in his next witness, he took a call from Dr Nakamura. The lab results were in.

'Any unusual findings?' he asked hopefully.

'All perfectly normal for a man of his age and medical history,' she said, 'Except for one thing. He had an abnormally large amount of oestrogen in his system. I can't account for it.'

'Female hormone?'

'Yes, but it is naturally present in the male body as well, and the amount fluctuates depending on diet, exercise, medication, things like that. But not a spike like this, that's very strange.'

'Could someone have introduced it deliberately?'

'It's possible, but why would anyone do that? In a large dose it might cause some discomfort, as any menstruating woman will tell you, but it isn't dangerous.'

'So it did not contribute to his death?'

'I cannot say.'

He started to reply, but she interrupted. 'No, sorry, but I can't. Perhaps his body reacted in an unpredictable way to the absence of his medication and a sudden hormone spike, but they could also be completely unrelated. There's no way of telling.'

He was about to hang up when a thought struck him.

'Dr Nakamura, what do contraceptive pills look like?'

'Little white or pink tablets, usually. Why?'

'The nurse said that Farndale never forgot to take his medication, and the family double-checked. Their first theory was that someone had substituted different pills. What if they are right? Only they didn't use something poisonous which would show up after death. They just made sure he did not get his medicine. Any little white pill would have done.'

'That is certainly a possibility, and it would explain the oestrogen.'

The only child of Victor's they hadn't spoken to yet was Mortimer Farndale, but he wasn't in, and instead of interviewing Juliette Westmacott, who was next on his list, Collins decided to return to the station to talk to Sergeant Holmes.

'Sally, where do women keep the pill?'

If she thought this a strange question, she didn't say. 'Bathroom cabinet, I suppose. That's where mine are. Or a bedside table or something.'

'Yes, they would, wouldn't they? Out of reach for children, but not actually under lock and key. Easy enough to get your hands on.'

'Agreed, but I don't see what you're getting at.'

He told her about Dr Nakamura's findings. 'Would it take a woman to think of that, do you think?'

She considered. 'It may be more likely, but it doesn't have to be. *You* thought of it. And Victor had already given them the idea of the substitution.' She shook her head. 'You know what bothers me about this? So Dr Nakamura thinks we cannot prove that this was done deliberately, even though things point in that direction. Fair enough. But what kind of murderer uses a method with only a middling chance of success? Victor could have noticed the difference in the pills. So could Eliza or the nurse. He could have survived for two or three days without his medicine and be right as rain when the new cycle started on Monday. The first responders could have revived him. If you wanted to get rid of him, wouldn't you want to make sure?'

'You're saying it is almost as if they were just giving it a try.'

'Or as if Victor's death would be convenient, but no big deal if it didn't happen.'

'You are right, that does seem strange.'

But before he could pursue that line of thought, his phone buzzed. Dr Nakamura again.

'I have just thought of something,' she said, 'In the scenario you have proposed – and please, please remember that I cannot confirm that is what actually happened – Mr Farndale would not have received his regular dose of medicine on Saturday night.'

'Yes.'

'And he usually took the tablets at around seven o'clock?'

'Yes, he kept closely to his routine.'

'Then the absence of the medicine on Saturday by itself was not enough to kill him. He died between eight and nine, the time is too short.'

'What are you saying?'

'I'm proposing – with all the due caveats – that Mr Farndale's pills had *certainly* been swapped before he took his morning dose and *probably* before his Friday evening dose.'

'Progress,' he told Sally, 'Dr Nakamura thinks the switch must have happened on Friday, so we can cross everyone who arrived late on Friday or on Saturday off the list.'

Sally leafed through Nora's timeline. 'Let's see, that means Matt, Bella, and Poppy. All Victor's own children were already there. Not a huge amount of progress, all told.'

Perhaps not, but he still thought that she was pleased that it meant that Matt Fielding was in the clear.

'And how do we know the switch did not happen days earlier?' she continued, apparently determined to make things as difficult as possible. He had an answer to that, though.

'Because the nurse visited on Friday morning, and she might have noticed something was wrong with the pills in that case. Our murderer took a calculated risk with their method, but I don't think they were prepared to take a bigger one. And waiting until Friday meant there were a lot more people around with access to Victor's rooms. One thing is certain though, this wasn't a spur of the moment thing. If it was murder, it was premeditated.'

Although they now had a concrete lead, the CID meeting the next morning was almost entirely given over to DI Graham's case. There had been another attack in the town centre on Thursday night, and there was no doubt now that this and the earlier incidents were related. Of course, the press had jumped to that conclusion already. They were calling the attackers 'the Butcher's Row Gang', which made the situation sound even more frightening than it was already for the people they targeted. Butcher's Row was the centre of a neighbourhood of pubs and bars, and people going home after a night on the town appeared to be the gang's preferred type of victim. In each instance, four unknown people had set upon a single person in an isolated spot, and beaten them up.

The first person to be attacked, two weeks ago, was Sylvester Murray, a twenty-eight-year-old investment banker on his way home from a stag do. He was drunk at the time when he was set upon, and hadn't been able to tell the police much about his assailants except that he thought there were four of them and they were wearing dark clothes with hoods. At the time they had treated it as an attempted robbery, although Murray still had his phone and wallet when he was found.

After the second attack it became clear that robbery was not the object. Samir Khan had been on his way to his job at the baker's on Market Street in the early hours of the morning, and although sober, could not improve on Murray's description much. There were four black-clad men, and their only apparent object was to rough him up.

'We were still prepared to entertain the possibility that the attacks were unrelated,' Graham said, mostly for DCI Dixon's benefit, 'That both Mr Khan and Mr Murray had a quarrel with someone and were not telling us everything they know. But last night's attack puts paid to that idea, I think. It is definitely the same MO.'

He put a picture up on the whiteboard.

'Conor Briggs, thirty-one years old. He's a big guy with gym-trained muscles, and he landed a blow or two on his attackers, but of course as long as we have no suspects we can't compare trace evidence.'

'Is there a connection with the other victims?' Collins asked.

'Robbins will be on to that later, but not at first glance, no. It doesn't look like the victims have much in common at all.'

'Well, they're all male,' DS Pardoe said.

'Yes, but that may just be a question of opportunity,' DS Holmes said, 'Girls on a night out stick together, they know they are more likely to get unwanted attention on their own. It is much easier to separate a man from the herd than a woman.'

'Good point, Sally.'

'They're doing it for fun,' Robbins said, 'Like football hooligans, or something. There's no point they want to make, they're just spoiling for a fight.'

DCI Dixon's eyes widened behind her large glasses as she looked at the DC. 'Don't be influenced by the press with their sensation-seeking. You cannot be sure that the attacks were deliberately planned. They may just be some drunken louts with poor impulse control.'

Graham came to Josh's defence. 'I believe it. Conor Briggs is the type with poor impulse control, he'd hit someone in anger, but there would be evidence all over the place. This is *organised*. If they were just some drunks we would have them in the cells already.'

'Do you think they're taking something to hype themselves up?' Sally asked.

'Possibly. But I'll bet you anything that at least one of them is stone cold sober all the time. Just look at the statements – they haven't slipped up once. They don't show their faces, they don't even speak, to the victims *or* to each other.'

'Which is what makes it so scary, of course,' Collins concluded, 'And so much fun for the headline writers at the Messenger.'

'And you have no suspects at all?' DCI Dixon asked, with what Collins regarded as unnecessary incredulity, 'What about CCTV?'

'Minimal,' Graham said, 'There's footage of the second attack, but it's too grainy even enhanced to make out individual features, and the camera covering the site of the first attack had been smashed the day before.'

'Coincidental?' the DCI asked.

'Or deliberate. Anyway, uniform are doing door to door in the area as we speak, but you know how it is around there in the middle of the night when everyone has been drinking. I'm not holding out too much hope. Trace evidence looks more promising. There was some blood on Mr Briggs's clothes that was not his, we'll run that through the database and hope we get a match.'

15

Matt Fielding was back at the station. Sally knew Collins had asked him to come in and provide more background now the investigation was official, so she wasn't surprised when he intercepted her in the reception area.

'Hey. Can I have a word? An unofficial one, I mean.'

'Sure.' she said, consciously casual.

'I didn't want to confuse things by going through the 'long time no see' rigmarole in the inspector's office. But it is good to see you, Sal.'

'You too. And I've told the DI that we know each other, you don't have to be secretive.'

'That's good. I didn't know where to look, the other day. I hadn't heard that you joined the police. But I think it suits you.'

'It does. So you won't be upset if I ask some searching questions?' she asked, showing him into the interview room.

'Bring it on.'

She had to stop herself from returning his smile. Stay professional, Sally, she told herself sternly. You're interviewing him, not meeting for drinks. She took the chair next to the DI and tried to assume a neutral expression suitable for listening to witnesses. She'd never actually thought about what she looked like during an interview before. Was this really the time to start?

'I was a foundling,' Matt explained, for DI Collins's benefit, 'I was literally left on the doorstep of St Bride's. They did everything they could to trace my family, but there was nothing to go on, just a piece of paper with my first name on it. No one had seen me being left. And so they looked after me. They couldn't arrange for an adoption as long as they still believed they could find out who I was, and later, when I got old enough, I resisted any attempts to find me a foster family. St Bride's was the only home I had ever known, and I didn't see why I should leave it. I don't think they tried very hard. There were always children who were in greater need of family care. And I like to think that, having known me from a baby, they were fond of me at St Bride's.'

He shot a brief smile in Sally's direction. He was right, she thought, they had been fond of him at the home, if only because he was no trouble.

'Someone once asked me whether I chose my field of study out of a desire for certainty and stability, which just goes to show how little the general public know about geomorphology. There is nothing so unstable as landscape, even without humanity making it worse. But it is true that I am always aware that I missed out on family life. That was one of the things I liked about life with Electra, that large family.'

'Had you been together long? And were you at Ulvercott often?'

'We met at a fundraising event at the university in September last year, about a month after Antigone and Simon got together. Electra first took me to Ulvercott for Victor's birthday later that month. I often came for weekends after that, but I rarely spent time with Victor alone. Until last weekend. He asked to see me, asked about my plans for the future, that kind of thing.'

'Why do you think he did that?'

'I can't be sure, but he could be old-fashioned in some ways. I think perhaps he wanted to make sure Electra would be looked after when he was gone. Of course, Electra is perfectly capable of looking after herself.'

'And you didn't tell Mr Farndale that you had doubts about your future with his daughter?'

'Of course not. I was only just beginning to realise that myself.'

'And you haven't told Electra this yet, either?'

'No. As you can appreciate there has hardly been an appropriate moment.'

'Then could you keep it that way for a little longer?'

Matt's eyes widened, but he agreed. 'If you think it will help.'

'I think it may. It would help if you could return to Ulvercott as you normally would, and keep an ear out for what the family discuss when the police are not there.'

'Why?' Sally asked Collins, as soon as they were out of the interview room, 'You've practically asked him to spy on them!'

'Because right now, he is about the only person we can be sure did not murder Victor Farndale. He arrived too late on the Friday, and if he isn't together with Electra he gains nothing by her father's death. But the others don't know that.'

'You're hoping the murderer will get overconfident.'

'Exactly.'

She had to admit that it could work, even though she would have preferred if Matt had been allowed to make a clean break with Electra. And why did she care so much about that?

After Mr Fielding had left, Rowena Dixon came to see Collins in his office. He and Sally had given her a brief rundown of the Farndale case after the meeting, and he had noticed then that she didn't look altogether pleased.

'Is it really necessary that you interview everyone yourself, Collins? You are a detective inspector, not a sergeant anymore.'

'I don't mind.'

If he was honest, he preferred it. He'd much rather be talking to people than sit behind a desk and delegate.

'It is not about whether you mind or not, it is about maintaining proper distinctions between ranks. You should be coordinating, not running after every witness yourself.'

'There isn't much to coordinate in this case, ma'am. And since we are a small team, everyone is used to pitching in where needed.'

She frowned. 'Yes, I really don't see how I'm supposed to manage with such a small department. I'm going to put in a request for two more constables as soon as I've got myself organised here.'

He didn't really see what she had to get organised, and he did wonder, if coordinating was *his* task, what DCI Dixon thought *she* was supposed to be doing. But he made a vague promise to behave more like an inspector, and then escaped to Ulvercott House as soon as her back was turned.

A very straightforward bloke, Mr Fielding, Collins thought, as they drove to Newbury Road to interview the remaining Farndales. So straightforward that he couldn't help thinking Matt must be holding something back. But even if he was, it wouldn't necessarily be anything to do with the murder. Most people kept something of themselves back all the time. Look at Sally and St Bride's – he hadn't known she had grown up in a home, and they had worked together for years.

They found that Mortimer had already left for work when they arrived at Ulvercott, and when Collins called Farndale Tech in Abbey Hill, they said that he was at a meeting with a client in another location, so he decided that Farndale's son could wait. Again. Mortimer's cousin Juliette was there, though, and happy to talk to them. She was the daughter of Ursula and Olivia's brother Peter.

'I went to school in France – my mother is French – but I always came to stay with Ursula in the holidays when I was a girl. And when I came to live in England after I finished university I started visiting again. I am the poor relation,' she added, 'They don't know they do it, of course, but the twins always make me feel it. Like last Friday: I arrived on the bus, and with changing trains at Newbury it is quite a journey. So Lecky says 'why didn't you drive?' I mean, she should know by now that my income doesn't stretch to running a car. Same thing when we go out, Lecky and Tiggy will always choose the place where a cup of coffee and a macaroon set you back a tenner. 'Come on, let's have lunch at the Radetzki.' They've no idea *at all*.'

It was a poor imitation of how Electra and Antigone talked, but she made her point. The Farndales were rich, and although Victor himself remembered what it was like to be poor, the same could not be said of his children.

'I mean,' Juliette said, warming to her theme, 'Lecky and Tig think they are slumming because they have jobs and pay for their board, but I couldn't see either of them sticking it in *my* job for more than a week.'

'And your job is...?'

'I'm an archaeologist. I'm giving a lecture at the Farndale Museum tomorrow, about what it was like around here in Roman times, or I wouldn't have hung around at all. This family gets on my nerves.'

16

'If the motive was money she's the other obvious candidate,' Collins said, when Juliette had gone.

'A bit too obvious, don't you think?' Sally said, 'Surely she wouldn't be in a hurry to stress her financial situation if she killed her uncle because of it.'

'Hm, yes, 'the poor relation'. There's some sort of history there. Did you notice that the others all call the twins by their full names? She is the only one who calls them Lecky and Tiggy,' he said thoughtfully.

'Childhood names, I suppose,' Sally said, 'Or a way to get back at them. Parents really should have more consideration. I bet they were called Leggy and Titty in school.'

'Probably. According to Ursula Annabel called all her children after plays she was in. She had played in a cycle of Greek tragedies before the twins were born, and she acted Isabella in *Edward II* when she was pregnant with Mortimer.'

Sally snorted. 'Some people shouldn't even be allowed near children.'

'It could have been worse.'

'How?'

He shrugged. 'Zenocrate? Oberon?'

'Yeah, right. How come you know so much about the theatre anyway?'

'I like plays, they have good stuff on at the city theatre sometimes.'

Sally's face indicated that she could think of better things to do with her spare time. 'Anyway, if we're not seeing Mortimer I'd better get back to the station. You can take Poppy on your own. I've had enough floppy-haired females to last me a lifetime.'

'Sure,' he said. Sally might not be as resentful as Juliette, but she clearly wasn't at home in the lap of luxury. And as soon as Poppy Alexander opened her mouth, he was glad his colleague wasn't there to hear her.

'I am training to become a wedding planner. I want to set up my own company.'

A wedding planner! He hadn't even realised that you could go to school for that.

'And you are engaged to be married yourself, to Oliver Farndale.'

'That's right,' she nodded.

She was very self-possessed for someone only just out of their teens, with her understated make-up and shoulder length blonde hair, like a girl in a TV commercial. He decided that his profession allowed him to put his foot in. 'Aren't you both a bit young for that?'

She didn't take offence. 'I know what I want, Inspector.'

That answered only half the question. Twenty- year-old women might know what they wanted, but in his experience that was rarely true of twenty-one-year-old men, even one as entitled as Robert Farndale's son. He hoped Poppy and Oliver were planning a long engagement.

'And you came here on Saturday to meet your fiancé's family?'

'Yes. I was so excited. Oliver had told me a lot about his grandfather, but I hadn't met him yet. He was very kind to me.'

'And the rest of Oliver's family? Do you know them well?'

'Not really, apart from Robert and Bettina. And Bella, of course. I thought Oliver's sister and I could be friends, but Bella is so immature, we didn't really hit it off.'

He could imagine. At that age, a difference of six years might as well be sixty. Poppy couldn't tell him much about the rest of Oliver's family, and coming from a wealthy home herself, could hardly be described as a gold-digger. He found it hard to imagine that she had anything to do with Victor's death.

'Can I go now, Inspector?'

'Just one more question, Miss Alexander. Are you on the pill?'

Before he could ask the other women in the house the same question, Sally called him from the station.

'I spoke to Eliza Farndale to ask about the solicitor who came to the house on Friday. It was Algernon Taylor, the retired partner from Taylor, Weir & Taylor. Apparently he sometimes saw Victor socially. They had known each other a long time, since his marriage to Olivia. And in Eliza's words, 'Victor wasn't one of those people who threatened to change his will all the time'.'

'Are we quite sure about that?'

Collins could hear the clicking of a keyboard in the background. 'I wouldn't know about the threatening, but the will held by Taylor, Weir & Taylor dates from just after Victor's third marriage. Fifteen years ago.'

'So if the motive was financial, it was a change in the murderer's, not the victim's, situation which prompted the attempt.'

'So we keep coming back to Robert,' she said.

'But he's been in trouble for a while, hasn't he? Why do it now?'

'Maybe because he didn't know how, before. Remember Eliza called him 'unimaginative'? Robert wouldn't have come up with the idea of the pills on his own, he needed the nudge from Victor himself.'

'That's possible. And he would have access to his wife's contraceptive pills, I suppose.'

But when he asked Bettina, she told him she had stopped using contraception years ago, with an expression that told him to draw his own conclusions about her marriage.

It was different again with the twins.

'The pill?' Electra asked, in the tones her mother would have used for *A handbag?*.

'Yes, Ms Farndale, I would like to know whether you and your sister use oral contraception,' Collins said patiently.

'Oh! You mean that was used to—' she broke off dramatically.

'We are investigating possibilities. If you could please answer the question...?'

'Why, yes, I use the pill. And so do you, don't you Tig?'

'In that case, could you both check if any are missing?'

When the twins returned, Electra told him that none of hers had been taken, but Antigone couldn't be so sure.

'I can be a bit slapdash about taking them, you see, I'm never on the right day. It could be that one or two are gone.'

Collins was briefly distracted by the idea that Simon Danvers might well father another unacknowledged child, but that wasn't his responsibility.

'Who could have had access to them, apart from yourself?'

'I keep them in my make-up bag, and that's usually in my bedroom. So Simon, I suppose. But it's not as if I lock my door. Anyone could have walked in. Juliette, Mortimer, anyone.'

Great. That didn't help. But if the murderer substituted Antigone's pills for Victor's heart tablets, at least six should be missing, not just one or two.

Of course, he had no way of knowing whether Electra and Antigone had told him the truth. Their surprise at his question could well have been acted. The problem was that most of what the twins said and did looked acted. He was beginning to see what Juliette meant when she said this family got on her nerves. Time to get out for a bit.

He was met in the hall by a man with a short dark beard and friendly brown eyes, dressed in the style Collins mentally classed as 'casual academic'. He'd become very familiar with it lately.

'Are you Inspector Collins? My name is Adam Rokeby. I wonder if I could have a word?'

'Ah, the new rector of St Oda's,' Collins said, holding open the door, 'But Ulvercott isn't part of your parish, is it? They belong to St Mary's in town.'

'I see my notoriety precedes me,' Rokeby said, sounding as if he was already a little tired of it.

'You were in the local rag. And I had a case at St Oda's at the end of last year. I suppose that story has preceded *me*?'

'The disappearance of Kester Johnson? Yes, I have been regaled with that. But to answer your question, I wasn't here in my professional capacity. Electra and Antigone and their brother are cousins of mine. I came to offer my condolences.'

'Of course! Annabel Rokeby. That's why your name seemed familiar when I saw it in the paper.'

'Exactly. Victor Farndale's second wife was my cousin. There wasn't much contact between the families after she moved down south, but I looked them up last week, after I was appointed at St Oda's. And when I heard the news of Victor's death I thought I should pay my respects.'

'I didn't think Victor Farndale was a religious man.'

'No, he wasn't. A confirmed atheist, in fact. His sister-in-law told me that that is why this is Ulvercott House now, instead of Ulvercott Abbey. But he wasn't one of those with a chip on his shoulder about it. I met Victor only once, although I have heard a lot about him with one thing and another, and he struck me as one of those people who are comfortable with the fact that others are not like themselves. That is quite rare, in my experience.'

'So he didn't mind you visiting?'

'Not at all. And in my job you get good at telling when you are not wanted.'

'As you do in mine, only we don't politely go away again.'

Rokeby smiled at that. 'I don't believe my cousins were all that happy to see me today, but I think Ms Westmacott was. Nice woman, coping with a lot at the moment, and I do not just mean her brother-in-law's death.'

'A murder inquiry is a lot to cope with,' Collins conceded, 'What did you want to speak to me about?'

'Not everything is about murder, Inspector,' Rokeby said, 'Although what I have to tell you may be. It's quite a story. Shall we go into the tearoom? I think I have trespassed on the Farndales' hospitality enough for one day.'

'Of course, I was just thinking I needed to be out of the house for a bit.'

They went into the lodge, and found a table overlooking the Newbury Road.

'Do you mind if I record this?' Collins asked, once they had been served their tea and scones.

Rokeby looked doubtful. 'It would be a bit like recording in the confessional.'

'It's for my personal use only. This is a complicated family, and I want to make sure I don't get things wrong and misremember. If you give us anything we need to follow up formally you will be asked to make a statement. This won't appear in court.'

17

Adam

I grew up in a small town in Yorkshire, where my family have farmed for generations. I won't say Annabel was the first Rokeby ever to leave, that can't be true, but it was certainly remarkable when she went to RADA in 1973. I wasn't even born then, but she was part of family legend, and knowing she had gone to live a very different life down south made it easier for me to do so when I grew up. If you type in Annabel Rokeby on YouTube you won't get many results, but she was famous in her day. She was a real stage actress, and played few television roles. She was best at the larger-than-life parts – Greek tragedy, or revenge plays. She called all her children after characters from plays she was in, and we used to joke that Mortimer was lucky he wasn't called Macbeth.

Annabel's father and my grandfather were brothers, twins. Fraternal twins run in the family. In my generation there's my cousins Joanna and Suzie, and of course Electra and Antigone. We didn't see much of Annabel after she moved to London and married Victor Farndale, but I got to know the twins after her death, when my mother looked after them for a while. As much as a young man of twenty can know a couple of distraught teenage girls, that is. And that brings me to why I wanted to talk to you. Electra and Antigone were thirteen at the time, and of course they were devastated at losing their mother. But there was something else as well. They had got it into their heads that their father had caused Annabel's death. Mam did everything she could to talk them out of the idea, but I don't think she completely succeeded. The twins calmed down after some time, adjusting to grief, as people do. They stopped believing in their own 'silly idea', or so they said. But I couldn't help but wonder. Mam might talk about how much their father had loved their mother, but she hardly knew the people in question, for all we knew there could be something in it. Not that I did anything about it, but I didn't forget it either. And now Victor Farndale himself has been murdered, and I wonder if there is a connection, if someone has finally had their revenge.

Not that I believe that Annabel was murdered. In our family no one was surprised that she was reckless with the stuff she took. But what matters is what others believe, isn't it? Specifically, what her children believe. I find it hard to imagine that one of those young women decided to end their father's life after all this time, unless something else has come to light in the meantime. On the other hand, if they made up their minds to do it, I believe there is some of their mother's recklessness in both of them. But you see why I am reluctant to share this with anyone else. It is your duty to consider possible suspects, but if there is nothing in this, I could do untold damage by casting aspersions.

I didn't actually talk about any of this during my visit, I couldn't find a way to raise the subject. You'd think a vicar would know how, but I found it hard to get a purchase on my conversation with my cousins. They seem to treat life as a play they are acting in. I didn't think introducing such a dramatic possibility would do much good. But I cannot ignore it, however unlikely. So there you are. A revenge tragedy, or much ado about nothing. I'll leave it to you to decide which it is.

18

'Where have you been?' Sally asked, when Collins returned to the incident room, 'I've been back here for ages. And who was Mr Tall-dark-and-handsome?'

'Sorry, something turned up. But you can cross that vicar who visited Ulvercott on Friday off our list. Did you see that piece in the Messenger about the gay rector? That was him. He wanted to talk, so I took him to the tearoom in the lodge.'

'But of course. You sure Mr Walsingham doesn't mind you going off with gay vicars?'

'Keep you mind on the job, Sergeant Holmes, sometimes tea is just tea. And he had something interesting to say about Farndale's second wife. Here.'

He put his phone down on the table between them and pressed play.

'He's very cautious,' she said, after listening to the recording, 'I like that.'

'His cousins are not half as scrupulous. Very eager to cast aspersions. Your Matt was right about that, at least, although it wasn't at him specifically.'

'He's not 'my' Matt, sir,' she said evenly, 'So what do we think? Electra and Antigone working together to finally avenge their mother's death? It would explain why they are both so eager to put the blame elsewhere.'

'Though not why they were the first to raise the possibility of murder. Wouldn't they have kept quiet instead, hoping for a verdict of natural causes?'

'I'm not sure they are capable of being quiet,' Sally huffed, 'Rokeby is right, it's all just a play to them. And all the others would have heard Victor at Christmas, so it would have been odd not to mention it.'

It all seemed to fit, there was opportunity, and a motive of sorts, but it didn't feel convincing to Collins.

'Of course there is the question of why they waited so long, unless it was Victor himself talking about the pills which gave them the idea,' Sally continued to think aloud, 'Or do you think they weren't sure until now and some new information came to light about their mother which set them off?'

'Or it may not have been the twins at all,' he suggested, 'What if Mortimer knew about this? Or Ursula.'

'Now there's a thing. Was there anything suspicious about the *first* wife's death?' Sally asked.

'Not as far as I know. She was on her way home late at night, alone in her car, and hit a patch of black ice on a bend. She hadn't been drinking, and wasn't speeding. What has that got to do with anything?'

'I just wondered, if her kids were right about Annabel's death, and now he has been married to Eliza for about the same time as he was married to her...'

'From what I have heard I find it hard to see Victor as a latter-day Bluebeard.'

'I agree. But is it the kind of thing a fourteen-year-old boy would imagine?'

'You think David offed his own father just in case?'

'Probably not. Anyway, if there were no questions asked about Olivia's death, and the suspicions about Annabel appear to have been entirely in her daughters' minds...'

He sighed. 'You're right. Hardly enough to build a case on, but I suppose we'll have to investigate. Is Mortimer back from work yet? We still haven't talked to him. And that's the last Farndale I want to see for now.'

'I'm a project manager with Farndale Tech,' Mortimer told them, 'The only one of the family still connected with the company. Although actually I only started working there after dad had retired and sold his share. There wasn't any nepotism involved. Or not in the way you'd think.'

'In what way then?'

'I've known Mr Mitchell, dad's old partner who runs the company now, nearly all my life, his son and daughter are mates of mine. So he may have put in a good word.'

'I see. And do you like your job?'

'Yeah, it's all right.'

Mortimer Farndale was halfway through his twenties, but he had the air of someone much younger about him, and Collins found himself automatically falling into the way of speaking he used with underage suspects. 'And at home? You get along all right with your family?'

'Yeah, sure. Why wouldn't I?'

'Well, with a father who has been married three times, I can imagine there could be tensions...'

Mortimer shrugged. 'Nah, I'm okay.'

'Okay,' Collins echoed. 'Let's talk about the events of last weekend. Where were you on Friday evening?'

'Playing FIFA with a couple of mates. I can give you their names, if you like. They'll confirm I was there.'

He was suddenly very eager to help, but Collins saw no reason to doubt his sincerity. The alibi could be checked easily enough.

'And do you have any idea who could have killed your father, and why?'

'It's obvious why someone would want to kill him, innit? We'll all be rich now.'

The attempt at toughness from the rich kid was almost comical. All the Farndale children had obviously been taught to enunciate clearly early in their lives, and he suspected the influence of their aunt Ursula's upper class tones as well as Annabel's theatrical projection. Mortimer might have picked up some expressions from his mates, but nothing that could disguise that he was as much a child of privilege as his siblings.

'Rich*er*,' Sally said.

'What?'

'You are all, with the possible exception of Juliette, extremely well off by most reasonable standards.'

'How do you know none of us has spent all their money on drugs, or betting, or something?' Mortimer countered.

'Because we check, of course,' Collins said.

He didn't add that those checks had revealed that Robert's business was in trouble and that Bettina wasn't getting as much freelance work as she liked to pretend. He wouldn't put it past them to favour Victor's death over, say, selling their country home or telling their son to get a job instead of living on his parents' money, but Mortimer did not need to know that. What he wanted to know was where Mortimer's own speculation led him. His twin sisters' opinions were extremely vocal, and Collins could imagine that Mortimer did not often get a word in edgewise, but that didn't mean he didn't have ideas, or that he hadn't seen anything. Eliza had called him secretive, and there was something watchful about his sullenness. No, not watchful. Wary. To Mortimer everyone was an enemy until proven otherwise. Something else they more often encountered in younger witnesses, or those of a lower social class.

'So if you believe the motive is obvious, who do you think is the culprit?'

Mortimer didn't answer at once, and Collins wondered if he was considering naming someone specific just because he disliked them. But in the end he was sure that Mortimer was honest, because he named the only person he knew all the Farndales were genuinely fond of.

'I think Aunt Ursula is hiding something. She hasn't been herself since dad died, and nothing has upset her so much before, not even mum dying. And I think she'd be capable of it, if she thought it was the right thing to do. But I can't think why. It's not as if she needs the money, and she doesn't get all that much, anyway.'

'Of course what Mortimer calls 'not all that much' may be plenty for others to do murder for, but I'm inclined to say he's right, and it is an unlikely motive for his aunt,' he told Sally afterwards.

'It's interesting that he says she hasn't been herself, though. None of the others have mentioned it.'

'No. But then, they are a self-centred crowd.'

'You are right there. But this means that Mortimer is off the hook for the murder, at least.'

'If his alibi checks out. He seemed a bit anxious about that.'

'That may just be because they all suspect each other. Everyone in this house recalls what Victor said last Christmas. They must all have made a guess as to who had taken up the suggestion, and know that others suspect them. They may be covering for each other as well, of course.'

'If it was Robert in an attempt to solve his financial problems, I don't see why the twins or Mortimer would cover for him. I don't get the impression they care for him much,' Collins said.

'It sounds like nobody does,' Sally conceded, 'But he is their brother – blood thicker than water, and all that.'

'That sounds like a foreign language, coming from you.'

She sighed. 'I wish we could eliminate someone. Anyone.'

'I'm pretty sure Poppy's innocent.'

'Great. Then we're down from sixteen to fifteen suspects. Let's get back to the station and report to the DCI.'

'But if his medication had been tampered with, isn't the nurse a person of interest?' Rowena Dixon said, when they put their findings before her.

Sally suppressed a sigh. Why was she even asking that? They had eliminated the nurse days ago, it was all on the system. But DI Collins answered as if it wasn't a stupid question.

'Her name is Katarzyna Krupinska. We interviewed her, and Robbins turned her records inside out, but there's nothing. She came to the UK at nineteen, started as a skivvy in a care home, did her nursing diploma, and has been working in the private sector since 2009. A few years ago she inherited enough money to put down a deposit on a house, but it wasn't a grateful patient, just a relative in Poland. And there is no suggestion that she benefits in any way from Farndale's death.'

'Does she know any of the family socially? If that oldest son is keeping her as his bit on the side...'

'Not unless he is a very good actor.'

'Why not?'

'Because he refers to Katarzyna as 'that Eastern-European woman'. You'd think if he was shagging her he'd know her name.'

'Man like that, not necessarily,' Sally put in, feeling that she wasn't really contributing to the conversation.

Collins shot her a warning glance, 'Be that as it may, what would she gain from murdering his father? And would a sensible woman like her use a method that points to the nurse as the first suspect? No, Katarzyna had nothing to do with it.'

'Speaking of records, did any of them have one?' DCI Dixon asked.

'Nothing apart from parking tickets. Well, and Nora Farndale has a conviction.'

'Really?'

'Bound over to keep the peace after an anti-vivisection demo in the early nineties. No bearing on this case, I think.'

'No, probably not. And you two have been conducting interviews at Ulvercott all this time?'

'Yes, the only ones we haven't seen yet are Bella Farndale and Simon Danvers.'

'Right, I see. Just do remember to keep your actions logged, will you? I like to know where my officers are. I'll see you both tomorrow.'

Sally made a face behind the DCI's retreating back, and turned to Collins.

'I mean, what are we, the bloody Met? There's a whole six of us, if Chandra ever gets back from his honeymoon, we're not likely to lose sight of what everyone else is doing, are we?'

'She just likes to feel she's in control,' Collins said, in what Sally considered an unnecessarily soothing tone.

Sally knew she wasn't being quite fair, and she knew she shouldn't bitch about Chandra getting married. She was happy for him and Bethany, she truly was. But when she had joined the CID three years ago, they had all been single except for Pardoe, who had been married for longer than Sally had been alive, and so didn't count. They used to go for drinks after work, they'd all been mates. Now Chandra was embarked on a life of wedded bliss, and Collie was living with Mr Walsingham, and if she suggested drinks, more often than not they declined. She'd never had many friends outside work, and there was no getting around it, she was jealous. She had never stuck it out longer than half a year with anyone, and couldn't imagine taking the leap Owen and Dominic had taken. Couldn't imagine it, but still wanted to. And now there was DCI Dixon to deal with, and Matt turning up...

Sally slapped her laptop shut and went home, alone.

19

Collins was surprised to see Rowena Dixon at the station on Saturday morning. There really wasn't anything urgent on that would require a DCI's presence during the weekend, he was only clocking in himself because he wanted to poke around at Ulvercott House some more.

'Collins, I wonder if the Farndale case really warrants so much expenditure of manpower. After all, the death may have been accidental. Culpable negligence rather than murder.'

'We would still need to investigate, if that were the case. But I am sure it was murder, ma'am. That is not in question. We may not be able to prove it, is all.'

She blinked at him from behind her glasses. 'I don't understand. If you cannot prove it, how can you be so sure?'

He had no idea what to say to that. Some people called it having a copper's nose, others said it was a gut feeling. The closest he could get was saying that he could see the shape of the case, and it looked like murder. It was something you learned only through spending years on the job. Graham had it, Sally was starting to develop it, Josh didn't even know it existed yet. But some coppers never developed that sixth sense for crime, and it looked as if Rowena Dixon was one of them. He took refuge in circumstantial evidence.

'There is the family's conviction that it is foul play. And Dr Nakamura agrees that it is the most likely scenario.'

'I see. Is there much chance of re-offending, do you think?'

'I would not say so. There was only one Victor Farndale.'

'In that case this is not our top priority. I want you to put this on the backburner until the assault case is resolved. I need all officers on that.'

'Has DI Graham asked for assistance?' As far as he knew Graham and Robbins were well on top of things.

'I decide who works on what here, not DI Graham.'

'Of course, ma'am.'

At his desk, he looked at the actions on the Farndale case, and wondered how to get them done without Rowena noticing. Under Bridget Flynn he had never hesitated to go off on a tangent when he felt a case demanded it, but going directly against a superior's orders was something else again. The DCI was probably right that a delay wouldn't make much difference to the investigation at Ulvercott House, but he hated to leave work half done. And he doubted very much that he and Sally would be much use to Graham at this point. What would they do, interview non-existent witnesses?

When he arrived at Ulvercott later, Collins was surprised to find Eden Kingston hoovering the hallway. He thought she had only come to help out just the once.

'You're a friend of Jake's, aren't you?' he asked, when she switched off the vacuum cleaner to say hello.

'Yes, we were in the same year at uni. Well, I'm still there, of course.'

'So what brought you to Ulvercott?'

'You recall that student job agency of Hugo Forrester's?'

He nodded. He was unlikely to forget about Odd Jobs, the company that had been at the centre of a sophisticated blackmail operation until a few months ago.

'Well, Isabel Norton is still running it,' Eden continued, 'I've been sent to help Jacqueline before. I was also here the weekend before last because they wanted to clear out the attic. And with a house this size that's a lot of work.

Jacqueline and I were up there for hours.'

'And you came last weekend when all the family where here. But today?'

'There are people coming to offer their condolences, and journalists trying to talk to the family, and Jacqueline is run off her feet. So I offered to come and help out again. And...' she hesitated and then said, with a disarming smile, 'And I'm a psychology student. I have to admit to professional curiosity. How often do you get to observe the reactions of a family when one of them is killed, and one of them is the killer? Call me a ghoul, but I'm fascinated.'

He liked her frankness, but he knew he shouldn't encourage it.

'You will be careful, though? Don't forget that to the killer this isn't a game.'

Eden went back to her work, and Collins went in search of Ursula Westmacott. As he climbed the stairs, he recalled Sally asking what kind of murderer used a method which wasn't sure to succeed. Perhaps he was wrong, and the killer *did* think this was a game.

When he found Ursula he asked her, as tactfully as he could, about the circumstances of Annabel Rokeby's death. It turned out the twins had not kept quiet about their suspicions at the time.

'And I think I know where the idea came from, too,' their aunt told him, 'I'm afraid Electra and Antigone made a habit of listening at doors, and one day they overheard a quarrel between their parents. Victor was remonstrating with Annabel about the prescription drugs she was taking, and he shouted at her 'It will kill you!' – I was *not* listening at doors, but he raised his voice enough that I came to see what was wrong, just in time to see the girls slinking away. When

I heard about that silly idea of theirs, I realised they thought they had heard him say '*I* will kill you'.'

'I see. And no one else shared Electra and Antigone's suspicions?'

'The coroner concluded that it was an accidental overdose, and knowing Annabel as we did, no one here ever thought otherwise. Victor was right, infuriating man, the drugs did kill her in the end.'

'Not suicide?'

Ursula looked at him, weighing her words. 'This is going to sound very unkind, but I think she would have made more of a performance of it in that case. And I don't believe she would have willingly left her children, not even in her most despairing moods. She took the pills to keep going, not to end it all.' She sighed. 'It was a terrible time. Robert and Nora were already grown up and had left home. But Mortimer was just ten and the twins were thirteen years old. There had been an au pair girl for a while when the girls were little, but at that time Annabel wanted to do all the mothering herself, and that worked well enough, since I was there to jump in whenever she was away. I don't think she ever realised how much work I took out of her hands. It would be easy to resent that, and sometimes I did, but you have to realise that Annabel was a very charming woman, and she meant well. It was hard to stay angry with her for long. By which I mean to say, she may have been hard work, sometimes, but no one would have wanted to murder her, and she was deeply mourned.'

Owen went straight home from Ulvercott House, not bothering to stop by the station, and wrote up his notes on his laptop. When he had finished, Dominic handed him his phone with a YouTube clip playing. 'Here.'

'What's that for?'

'You've been singing 'Eleanor Rigby' for two days, and you clearly don't know the words. I found you a video with the lyrics.'

'Have I?' He hadn't been aware of it himself. He knew he had a tendency to hum along with whatever background music was playing, and sometimes the songs got stuck in his head, but he couldn't recall hearing the Beatles recently. Then he had it.

'Of course. I've been thinking about Annabel Rokeby.'

'Is she to do with your case?'

'I'm not sure. She was Victor Farndale's second wife.'

'Wait— Rokeby? Wasn't that the name of the gay rector?'

'Yes. He's a second cousin. I met him yesterday, in fact. Nice bloke.'

Dominic raised an eyebrow. 'Fast work. Why exactly did you meet him?'

'Keep your imagination in check. He came to offer his condolences to the Farndale family, and I took the opportunity to ask him some questions about Annabel. She died of an overdose, and Victor's first wife died in a car accident.'

'*To lose one wife may be regarded as a misfortune; to lose two looks like carelessness*?'

'Something like that. Anyway, there's probably nothing in it, but I do have to ask the questions.'

Owen knew he really shouldn't be talking about the case so much, so he was glad when Dominic changed the subject.

'I saw Jake in town today. He was on reception at the Radetzki, of all things.'

'Yes, he's still on the books at Odd Jobs, Eden Kingston told me. I think he likes not being tied to a single job.'

'We should invite him and Noah to dinner sometime,' Dominic suggested.

'That would be nice. Are they at the stage where we can invite them as a couple?'

'We can always ask one each and then act surprised when they turn up together.'

He smiled. 'Of course. Seriously though, are those two all right?'

'Given that Jake's been suffering from clinical depression and Noah is terminally shy, I think they are doing brilliantly.'

Dominic looked at him when he didn't say anything. 'I mean it, you know. Jake's fine. You don't have to worry about him all the time now.'

That was true, but it was a habit that was hard to break. Dominic was right though, Jake had been doing well over the last few months, since he had quit the university, and especially since he met Noah Rosenthal, one of Dominic's graduate students. It was an unlikely pairing in some ways, which was why he couldn't help being a little apprehensive. Dominic appeared a lot more confident.

'I think I'll ask them for Sunday week. You're unlikely to be working on a Sunday, are you?'

'That should be fine,' he agreed, 'What were you doing at the Radetzki anyway?'

'Meeting the editor of the university press. I'd be happier in the campus coffee shop, but I think she's got delusions of grandeur.'

Owen pictured the Radetzki, the town's most opulent grand hotel. 'If Jake was on reception, was he wearing one of those bellhop uniforms of theirs? With the short jackets?'

Dominic nodded. 'And the frogging. It looks like something that should be regulated by law. The Obscene Publications Act, possibly.'

20

'It's all on the system,' Collins concluded his summary of the Farndale case for the CID meeting on Monday morning. It had been a week since Matt Fielding had come in with his story, and it didn't feel as if they had made much progress at all.

'The system? Why can't you just call it by its name?' DCI Dixon said irritably.

Sally pulled a face behind the DCI's back.

'Well, ma'am, if you have an officer called Holmes, it just sounds wrong. So we usually just call it the system.'

And because it is a stupid name, he added silently. The people in charge were obsessed with creating a modern, efficient, fully automated police force. They had developed a sophisticated computer system to help handle the challenges of policing in the age of information technology. And then they called it HOLMES, after the brilliant maverick who solved crimes without recourse to any police methods whatsoever. To Collins it suggested that, management-speak notwithstanding, the leading lights of Her Majesty's constabulary were more than a little in love with their fictional image.

Not that he had anything against HOLMES 2, it was very useful. But Rowena Dixon appeared to think the system solved crimes all by itself. It was true the database made it much easier to recognise patterns. But you could only recognise patterns that were there. Their case, with a single victim, a limited set of suspects, and what was probably a first-time offender, didn't benefit much from the available information.

They had dutifully pursued the forensic evidence, but the hair found in the medicine box had turned out to be Katarzyna's, and the wool fibres couldn't be identified without a source to compare them to. Sunita Mahajan's gloves weren't a match, and there did not appear to be any other pairs of dark blue ones at Ulvercott House.

'So you have nothing,' Rowena concluded.

For someone priding herself on her positive attitude she could be surprisingly discouraging.

'I wouldn't say that, ma'am. We have some persons of interest with motive and opportunity, and we are pursuing several lines of inquiry.'

Collins knew it was unfair to keep comparing Rowena with DCI Flynn. But he also knew that Bridget would never have let such a vague assurance slip past unnoticed.

'Several lines of inquiry?' Sally asked sweetly, when Rowena had gone back into her office.

'We'd better find some hadn't we? Let's get back to Ulvercott.'

Was it strange that DCI Dixon hadn't said anything about Sally's surname? Collins wondered as the DS drove them to Farndale's house. It could just be that Rowena realised that Sally had had it up to here with great detective jokes and people asking her where Watson was, but it was almost as if the name simply didn't register with their new boss. Collins met plenty of people on whom literary references were wasted, but surely everyone had at least seen *Sherlock* on TV? Even Victor Farndale had it on DVD.

Collins recalled DC Holmes three years ago, fresh out of uni and looking even younger, being introduced to Bridget Flynn.

'It's a bold choice, wanting to become a detective with a name like that,' the DCI had said, 'But I suppose you can't help your father's name now, can you?'

'It's my mother's name actually, ma'am,' Sally had replied stoically.

'Why on earth are you using your mother's name?'

Sally had waited a beat and then said. 'My father's name was Bond.'

That wasn't true, of course – Sally went by her mother's name because she did not know who her father was. But it made the DCI laugh, and the moment had created a natural rapport between Bridget and the young constable, one which Rowena was signally failing to recreate.

When they arrived at the house, they met Adam Rokeby just going out. Collins waved for Sally to go inside without him and stopped to talk.

'Visiting your cousins again?'

'No, I came to see Ms Westmacott. A pastoral visit, nothing criminal, in case you wondered.'

Collins thought Rokeby was a bit too eager to reassure him of that, but he let it go for now. 'Of course. How are you settling in? Any more trouble with the reactionaries?'

'It's not as bad as all that. To tell you the truth, I think most people have more trouble with my accent than with me being gay. And you can tell most of them are simply glad to have a rector again. I'm told that before I came here the parish has been through a rather turbulent time.'

'That's a way of putting it. How is Gabriel Butler doing?'

'Coping. His daughter is a great help.'

They chatted some more, until Collins realised that he was doing exactly what Rowena feared he did when she wasn't watching, being distracted by things that had nothing to do with the case. He had witnesses to question. Specifically, he wanted to know what Jacqueline Whyatt knew about the circumstances of Annabel Rokeby's death. The housekeeper must surely see more than anyone else of what went on in the house.

Sally found Electra and Antigone both at home and free to talk to her. Didn't these women work?

Without revealing their source, she put it to them that they might have a motive for their father's murder.

'That old story...' Antigone said, 'You surely can't think that has anything to do with this. And whoever told you?'

'I think we really believed it for a while,' Electra continued, without giving Sally a chance to reply, 'I suppose it was easier to live with than the idea that one's mother had died through her own carelessness. I was very angry with her, we both were, for leaving us.'

Antigone nodded her agreement to this. For a moment the bubbly attitude deflated, and there were only two tired, rather unhappy women sitting there.

'At the time, you both alleged that Victor had threatened her. That you had heard him say 'I will kill you',' Sally said bluntly, refusing to feel pity for the twins, of all people.

'You know, I had forgotten all about that. I do remember him shouting at her. That was unusual, they didn't have big rows as a rule. But I really couldn't tell you now if he said that. Young girls imagine things,' Electra said.

'You should hear the things Bella comes out with,' Antigone added.

'According to your aunt, what Victor said was '*it* will kill you', referring to the drugs she was taking.'

'Well, there you are then. Mystery solved,' Electra said brightly.

'Not quite. Because someone *did* kill Victor. Do you think there was anyone else who believed him to be responsible for your mother's death? Your brother, perhaps?'

'Mortimer? I can't imagine. We never talked to him about it, he was too young,' Antigone replied, 'And there's no else who cared so much about mum.'

Sally thought that that wasn't quite true. Ursula Westmacott had clearly been very fond of Victor's second wife. Fond enough to avenge her death? Sally wouldn't put it past the old lady.

'How was your day?' Dominic asked, when Owen came home from another round of inconclusive interviews.

'I had an interesting conversation with Adam Rokeby about the place of the church in modern society.'

'Is that copperese for 'I'm not allowed to talk about the case'?'

Was it? In his last two murder cases, Dominic had been to a certain extent involved (which was worrying on an entirely different level), and if Owen hadn't kept him in the loop someone else would have. But Dominic did not know the Farndales at all, and that meant he had to think about what he could and could not talk about at home.

'The victim's daughter's fiancé – or ex-fiancé – is an old mate of Sally's. It was he who came to us with the case in the first place. I think it has upset her a lot more than she's saying.'

'DS Holmes has always struck me as a tough young woman.'

'She is. But we all have our breaking point. And on top of this she doesn't get along with DCI Dixon at all.'

'And do you?'

He shrugged. 'It's too early to tell.'

Dominic looked at him as if he were a student who had failed to hand in an essay on time. 'Owen, you are capable of making friends with a suspect after twenty minutes in an interview room. If you are unsure whether you like someone after a whole week of working together, the answer is probably no.'

21

He certainly wasn't going to be friends with this one, he thought the next morning.

'And what if he did?' Gareth Swift asked, when requested to confirm that Mortimer Farndale had spent Friday evening with him and his friends, playing video games. Swift wasn't surly, or defensive, the way even innocent people tended to be when questioned by the police. He just gave the impression he wasn't particularly interested one way or another, lounging on his sofa as if he had all the time in the world. He hadn't, he worked fulltime at Farndale Tech, which was how he knew Mortimer.

They were in Swift's flat above a shop in Court Street, but it was almost as if he was interrogating a suspect at the station instead of just asking a witness to confirm a detail. All his alarm bells were going off, telling him that Swift was an unscrupulous and egotistic liar. But one who was, on this occasion, probably simply telling the truth. Like Scott and Tash Mitchell, he confirmed that Mortimer had been with them from late afternoon through the evening on Friday. Scott and Tash had gone home, but Mortimer had slept on Swift's sofa, making it very unlikely that Victor's son was the one who had tampered with the pills. Collins had the idea that if Mortimer had slipped away at any time during the evening, Swift would have happily dropped him in it.

'Will that be all, Inspector?'

'Thank you, Mr Swift, if there is anything else we'll be in touch.'

'You know where to find me.'

That shouldn't have sounded like a threat, but it did. Collins would be happy if he never saw Gareth Swift again. Still, another person of interest less on the list. If they were lucky, they might get there eventually simply by a process of elimination.

While Collins was checking Mortimer Farndale's alibi, Sally drove to Overdene House to speak to his niece. She was glad to get away for a bit, to be honest. She knew it wasn't rational, but they were only one week in and already she couldn't stand her new boss.

Rowena Dixon appeared to consider it part of her job description to deliver little motivational speeches whenever she set foot in the CID room. This morning it had been all about 'pulling in the same direction', and she wouldn't let them get on with their work until they had all individually agreed that this was a good thing. Sally didn't think it was necessarily a good thing at all. She didn't get why they had to agree all the time. In any job you sometimes had to do things you would have done differently if you were in charge. That didn't mean they all mutinied when they disagreed with the DCI, it just meant they sniggered quietly when said DCI ended up with egg on her face. They didn't need to be motivated to perform their actions, let alone convinced. And they didn't need to think the same way about them. Different approaches in detective work tended to help rather than hinder, a concept DCI Dixon appeared not to have come across in her career to date. But Sally knew from experience that it was true. She tended to be suspicious, Collins was more trusting. Sometimes she reminded him that not everyone had the best intentions, and at others he was the one to tell her that not everyone had ulterior motives. It was a good combination, just like DI Graham's experience and Josh's need to learn combined well. If they all thought the same way they'd never get anywhere. And that made the noses-in-the-same-direction sessions pretty useless, didn't it?

Of course, it could be said that a trip to a girls' boarding school wasn't much of an escape, she thought, as Overdene House hove into view. She wondered if Rowena Dixon had attended a place like this. Sally, of course, had been educated at the local comprehensive, and considered herself none the worse for that. Overdene House had navy blazers and pleated skirts, acres of playing fields, and a list of famous alumni as long as your arm. Sally was hating it already.

She identified herself through the entryphone at the gate and asked for Tara Saunders, Bella's housemistress.

'Are you thinking 'it looks almost like a real school'?' the latter asked, as she led Sally through a corridor of classrooms.

Sally had to admit that that was close.

'You came all prepared to disapprove, didn't you? Believe me, I know where you're coming from with that. But really all we try to do here is give them the best education we can, academically and as individuals. The trappings are just for the parents.'

'I grew up in a home. I was thinking 'it looks just like a bunch of kids living together'.'

Sally surprised herself by saying that so easily. She didn't even know this woman! But Ms Saunders wasn't at all what she expected. Younger, for one thing, and not at all condescending.

'And that's exactly what they are. Sweet girls most of the time, trouble occasionally.'

'And does Bella Farndale ever give you trouble?'

'No more than you would expect from a fifteen-year-old. She's one of our best athletes, and academically very bright. Don't be fooled by her apparent inability to string two words together, they all sound like that. Bella is a clever girl. But emotionally, I would say she is still very much a child. And very literal-minded.'

'Does she talk about her family much?'

Ms Saunders had to think about that. 'Families are a sensitive subject. You remember when you thought everything your parents did was too embarrassing for words? Or... Sorry, you said a home, so perhaps not.'

'You think that doesn't apply to paid staff? I would have died rather than be seen with Miss Gardiner that time when she had her hair dyed.'

'Yes, that's the principle I mean. Well, Bella's grandfather married his third wife around the time she was born, with the result that she has an uncle who is younger than herself. I don't think she is too eager to have the other girls know about that. They can be cruel about things they consider not 'normal'. But I don't get the impression Bella doesn't get on with her family.'

Ms Saunders left Sally outside a classroom door and came back a moment later with a girl who looked no different than any of the others. That old-fashioned uniform, shoulder length blonde hair, vacant supermodel stare. Sally identified herself, and noticed a spark of interest in the girl's eyes, before it was replaced again by boredom.

'I was at Ulvercott on the Friday because I'd left my hockey things there over Christmas,' Bella explained, 'And we had a match on Saturday – I'm on the first team. It was no bother, we had the afternoon free, and the bus stops just by the gates. Of course I ran into Aunt Ursula and she scolded me about being forgetful, but it wasn't like I was anywhere I shouldn't be. I didn't see anyone else except Juliette, she was smoking on the terrace.'

'So you were at Ulvercott briefly on Friday, and then you came back on Saturday afternoon. Do you get on well with your family? With your grandfather?'

'Not really. He thought I was silly. I heard him tell Nora. I suppose he wanted me to become an ugly cow like her. As if!'

'Bella!' Ms Saunders said. Sally didn't like the interruption, but she had to hand it to her, until that moment she had forgotten the schoolmistress was even there.

'Sorry, Ms Saunders,' the girl said, not sounding contrite at all. 'Anyway, I don't think grandfather liked *me* very much, but that's hardly why someone killed him, is it? Have you got a theory yet? Because it won't be any good, you know. Not the first one, *or* the second. The police never get anywhere until after they've arrested their third suspect.'

'I think you've been watching too many episodes of *Vera*,' Ms Saunders said, 'Will that be all, Sergeant? I think Bella should go back to her class.'

'Crime dramas?' Collins asked, when she called him to report on her conversation with Bella, 'Is that a normal thing for a fifteen-year-old girl? I thought they all watched things about vampires and werewolves.'

'And since when are you an expert on the taste of fifteen-year-old girls?'

'Well, is it?'

'No, I suppose not. More the kind of thing her mother would watch. Perhaps it's a mother-daughter thing.'

'Perhaps. I'll ask Bettina.'

'Are you at Ulvercott then?'

'Just got here. I've spoken to Gareth Swift, and Scott and Tash Mitchell. Mortimer's alibi stacks up.'

'Shame.'

'I also spoke to Ursula. There will be a memorial for Victor held in the cathedral on the twenty-third.'

'In the cathedral? I thought Victor was an atheist?'

'He was, apparently that's why it's not called a memorial *service*, but it's still the most convenient place for something like that. We've been focusing on the family, but he was an influential and a well-liked man, there will be hundreds of people there.'

'Are you going?'

'Of course.'

He called her back half an hour later, when she was nearly home.

'Bettina says watching crime series was something Bella and her grandfather had in common. *Sherlock*, *Vera*, *Broadchurch*, they both watched them all the time. Apparently Bella likes to point out where the scripts get it wrong. Bettina says she must have been thrilled to be speaking to a real-life detective.'

Thrilled was not the word Sally would have chosen for Bella's reaction. But then, she had probably been perpetually bored herself at that age. She really shouldn't read too much into the girl's hostility. Her relationship with her grandfather had obviously been better than she admitted, if they binged on *Sherlock* together.

22

Owen had just put the phone down, full of a new idea that had come to him after talking to Bettina yesterday, when he was ambushed by Rowena Dixon.

'Collins, I know you two are thick as thieves, but I want to talk to you about Sally's attitude. Is she quite professional enough?'

'How do you mean, ma'am?'

'I can't help noticing that she is sometimes a little... disrespectful towards her colleagues. I wonder about her behaviour towards witnesses.'

'I have never seen her other than professional, ma'am. But of course you can observe the interviews at the station yourself.'

'Yes, I shall do that, if you ever get to the point of bringing someone in. As for her general conduct, I think she would benefit from DI Graham's example. On the next case, I shall assign her to him, and you can work with DC Robbins.'

He stared at her. She had just as good as told him that he was a bad influence, but she did not appear to be aware of it herself. She blithely continued about her assessment of the rest of the team and where she saw room for improvement.

'Where have you been?' DS Holmes herself asked, when he returned to the CID room. 'I could have done with some help putting all this on the system.' She waved a hand at their notes of yesterday's interviews.

'DCI Dixon wanted a chat about the team.'

'So? We're doing all right aren't we?'

'Apparently. I've just been told that we are 'a great mix from a diversity angle'.'

'What, and you always thought that you got where you are now on merit alone?'

He glared at her. 'Just remember that, however I got there, I am in a position to give you a bollocking for insubordination.'

Sally just grinned.

He looked at Peter Graham, 'Seriously though, if that is what the DCI means when she says she is assessing the team...' He would have bet good money that Graham had got where he was because he was a good copper, not because he was black.

Graham shrugged. 'Don't be too hard on her, they get told to do that from higher up. They're falling over backwards to be inclusive, it's no wonder they sometimes miss the point.'

Josh Robbins came into the CID room at that moment.

'Oh look, it's our token straight white male,' Sally said cheerily.

DS Pardoe cleared his throat loudly.

'Sorry, Pardoe, didn't see you there.'

'Have I missed something?' Robbins asked, looking from one to the other.

'Only our dear DCI putting her foot in. Right, I'm off, I need a break,' Sally said.

Robbins looked a question at DI Graham.

'Never you mind, lad. Just get going on your actions.'

'Right, guv.'

'Guv?' Collins said, as he followed Sally out, 'He never calls *me* guv.'

She shrugged. 'I suppose neither of us lives up to Josh's image of the ideal copper – or Rowena's. Where are we going, anyway? I just needed an excuse to get out.'

'Yes, so did I,' he said absentmindedly, as they walked down Petergate together.

'Sir?'

'Hm? I'm thinking about dead fish.'

'Just in general, or specific dead fish? And could you walk a little slower, please?'

He collected himself and slowed down.

'We agree that the killer substituted contraceptive pills for Victor's medicine, right? And once they had swapped the pills they would have needed to get rid of the superfluous tablets. Assuming it happened on Friday and they switched those for Saturday and Sunday as well, that means six of them. Easy enough to flush down the lavatory, if you didn't want them to be found in the bin. But I don't think that's what they did.'

He told her about the fish he had seen floating in the pond. 'What if someone threw the pills in there and they gobbled them up?'

'It's possible. Can we test the fish? It would be another piece of circumstantial, at least, if they turn out to have Victor's medication inside them.'

'No luck there. I just called Ulvercott, but the gardening firm come on Thursdays and they disposed of the dead fish. But that wasn't what I was getting at. Why bother to go into the garden to get rid of the evidence in the first place?'

Now she understood.

'Because they weren't supposed to be in the house at all? Or not yet? We've been looking at the people who were there on Friday, but you think we should be looking at those who weren't.'

'Yes. It would be easy enough to approach the house without anyone noticing. The west wing isn't in use, and most of the family were in one of the front rooms. There wouldn't be that big a risk of being seen. It would still probably be someone close to the Farndales, but I think we need to take a look at the ones who say they weren't there on Friday afternoon.'

Sally didn't need to look at the timeline anymore. 'That means Mortimer and Poppy are back in the frame. And Matt.'

'But Matt says he was in Southampton until five, that should be easy enough to check with his colleagues. It would be a squeeze to drive to Ulvercott in time to slip in before it was time for Victor to take his pills. Let's concentrate on Robert's family and Mortimer for now. Have you cooled down enough to return to the station?'

Sally agreed that she had, but she was lying. She was hot and edgy, not with the familiar rush of being on the trail, but with fear that Matt could be in the frame again.

When had it happened? Where was the point when it had became so important to her that Matt Fielding was innocent of this crime? She hadn't noticed, she only knew that right now, it was. She needed Matt to be innocent. She needed Matt to be sensible and down-to-earth, with his old dry humour and tolerance of other people's foibles. She needed him to be the Matt she had once known, not the devious, calculating gold-digger as described by Antigone. Because falling in love with a criminal was really sinking too low, and whichever way she looked at it, she couldn't deny that she was falling in love with Matt.

She jumped at every chance to accompany Collie to Ulvercott, just because Matt might be there (only to find him together with the woman he said he was not dating anymore, of course). She had no idea whether he felt the same. The Matt she remembered didn't wear his heart on his sleeve, and he was up to his ears in a murder investigation. He had other things to think about. Possibly the smile he gave her when they met was just relief at seeing a familiar face. It was still a very nice smile, though. And an honest one, surely?

'Mortimer Farndale says he was playing FIFA with his mates on Friday till late, and they all confirm that,' Collins said when they were back in the CID room, 'I've spoken to a Mr Swift, and to the Mitchells.'

'I wonder what they were really doing all night,' Sally said absently.

'Why do you think they were doing something other than what they say?'

She straightened up. 'These guys are about my age, right? And I'm supposed to believe they get together on a Friday night just to play fake football?'

'Happens more than you think. Apparently some of them are more serious about the computer version than about the real game,' Collins said.

'That's right,' DI Graham added, 'My son plays Football Manager all the time, it's like it is more real to him than actual football on a pitch. We used to go to matches at Dean Court when he was little, but now he'd rather stick to the screen.'

'You can even play FIFA competitively,' Josh said, 'There's tournaments and everything.'

Sally looked at her colleagues. 'You're taking the piss, right?'

The three men all shook their heads.

'Right. We live and learn, don't we? So Mortimer arrived at Swift's place, they phoned for pizza, and he played fake football with his mates until the small hours. And he was at work before that?'

'He was home for half an hour between work and leaving for Court Street, in which he showered and changed. He could have nipped downstairs to Victor's rooms, but no one saw him, and the house was pretty full by then.'

'Okay, so possible but not likely.'

'Yes, and that about goes for all of them.'

By the afternoon, Owen's enthusiasm for his own new idea was waning fast. He was looking through the statements from the tearoom staff, but the lodge overlooked only one approach to the house, and they hadn't seen anyone suspicious. And if one of the Farndales had arrived unexpectedly, they wouldn't look suspicious at all, would they? At least Matt Fielding's students confirmed that he had been in Southampton until past five, Sally would be glad to hear that. He had noticed her pretending not to care.

'How's your case coming along, Graham? Are you going to beat us to it?' he asked, to distract himself.

'I wish. You know as well as I do what you get when most of your witnesses were drunk at the time of the incident. Conor Briggs was lucky that someone was sober enough to call an ambulance straight away.'

'And the CCTV's no good?'

Graham gave him a look that said everything. 'I've asked uniform to increase their presence in the area, but you know what a warren it is. We're basically waiting for the next incident to happen.'

Before Collins could come up with something encouraging to say to that, the desk sergeant sent in a visitor. A young man who had been here before, and who bore a striking resemblance to his friend Jake.

'Inspector Collins? I've come to make my statement. And I brought something you might want to see. I know it's not evidence, for all you know I could have made it up yesterday. But it is the best account of last weekend I can offer.'

He put a ruled notebook on the desk. 'My counsellor said I should keep a journal. So I dutifully wrote down my impressions of the weekend. I don't think there is anything useful in there, but you had better be the judge of that. Only...'

'Yes, Mr Danvers?'

'I would be grateful if no one else read it.'

'Of course. As you say, it is not evidence. I'll make sure it stays private, Mr Danvers.'

He did this by taking it home to read, which meant explaining to Dominic what he was working on, and making him laugh at Sally's reaction on learning about FIFA-tournaments.

'And Rowena, is she getting easier to get along with?'

'She's on top of the assault case all the time, while Graham has that all in hand. It isn't his fault that there are so few leads. But she really wants me and Sally on that as well. I'm getting the feeling that Victor Farndale gets low priority because he was old and would have died soon anyway. Which rather misses the point of a murder investigation.'

'But surely she must have led murder investigations herself when she was a DI.'

Owen shrugged. 'I think Sally would agree that a good sergeant hides a multitude of sins. But then, she can't stand DCI Dixon. And it's not just Sally. I've already heard Josh refer to her as Miss Ravenclaw.'

'Miss...? Oh, from Harry Potter.'

'Exactly. It's hardly a sign that he is taking her seriously. Of course, it doesn't help that she sounds as if she has swallowed a management manual.'

'And are you getting anywhere with the Farndale case?'

'Oh, you know. Two steps forward, one step back. We could do with something to help us along. A witness would be nice. In both cases, actually. You'd think with an attack outside Bitters at closing time, someone would have seen something.'

'Yes, you would. And that reminds me, I've asked Noah and Jake for dinner on Sunday.'

'I like the way your mind works.'

'Well, my first meeting with Jake at Bitters *was* rather memorable.'

23

Simon

Extracts from the private journal of Simon Danvers

August 21
Carlotta said I should keep a journal, but I don't quite understand what it's supposed to do. I don't have to talk about what I write during my sessions, she says it's just for myself. I think she believes I'll put my innermost thoughts down here, things I daren't even say to her, but I don't think I have any of those. Just things it would be a bit embarrassing to talk about, like, my father is living with my ex, and I'm pretty sure their baby is half my baby. There. Writing it down didn't change anything, did it? I still don't know what to do about it. I mean, I'm not going to do anything about it, I don't want a child, particularly, and I'd rather forget about Claire. It's just, I'd like to know.

September 6
This writing business is beginning to grow on me. Maybe it's in my genes, mum's a writer, after all. And Jake says he wants to be one. I keep coming back to this, even though I don't have much to say, really. Although now there is Tig, so at least I have something cheerful to report. Carlotta says I shouldn't base my sense of self-worth on finding the right woman, but this isn't like the last time. Tig is very different from Claire. Not so serious all the time. Of course when I was with Claire I was also being serious all the time. It is strange being on

my own and never having to think about the rest of the family like I used to. Tig also has a large family, she's taking me to Ulvercott, her father's house, for his birthday.

December 27
There was an odd scene at Christmas dinner – the only time when Tig's father joined us downstairs – when Eliza brought him his pills and he showed them to the kids and explained that he couldn't survive without them. I think he was intending to be educational, not sensational, but it led to a discussion of how easy it was to slip someone something lethal. It reminded me of grandfather and uncle Solly. I wish Tig wouldn't be so flippant about such things. Although she isn't as bad as Juliette or Bella. That kid is positively ghoulish.
The rest of the evening was very nice, though. Electra had brought her fiancé, who's a geologist or something, and we had a round of poker with Olly and Mortimer.

February 2
Victor had a heart attack last Saturday. The ambulance came but they couldn't save him, it all happened very quickly.
Eliza went with him into hospital and as soon as she returned and told us what happened the others started crying murder. He was seventy-two and he had a bad heart. I couldn't see what they were all getting so upset about. I mean, obviously I can see that it would upset anyone if their old dad died, I would be upset if my dad suddenly packed it in, but I couldn't see why they thought it had to be foul play. (Do people still use the phrase 'foul play'? It's what Tig and Electra meant, anyway.) I thought they were all enjoying it way too much, Bella and the twins especially, but now it turns out they are right, apparently the police are taking it seriously. Tig says

Jake's friend DI Collins turned up at Ulvercott today. I suppose that means I'll have to talk to him, although I don't see how I can help.

Later.
I think Tig and her sister suspect me of having something to do with Victor's death. They haven't actually said, but they haven't said it very loudly.
Of course Tig will be rich now. I hadn't thought about that before. I wonder how rich? Victor was a millionaire, but so was my grandfather, and after death duties and divvying it up between us, you're not exactly talking never having to work again. It would make a difference to someone like Juliette, I suppose, or Matt. I don't like this at all. Apparently Eliza doesn't benefit at all, financially. I wonder whether she and Victor had a row or something? But you don't kill someone just because you disagree with them. Not unless you are like my grandfather. I don't like it that this is all happening again. I thought with Tig things could be normal. I suppose I'd better make a new appointment with Carlotta.

24

When he had finished with the journal, Owen called Sally at home. He knew she didn't really mind discussing a case outside working hours. Like he had before he met Dominic, she tended to be on the job 24/7.

'We haven't really looked at Eliza Sanford, have we? Are we sure she is telling the truth about her marriage?' he said.

'I suppose she could have come back to Ulvercott in her tea break, but we haven't caught her out in anything which contradicts the others' accounts,' Sally said, not sounding convinced.

'Robert had her down as the most likely suspect from the start, though.'

'Well, one thing they all agree on is that Robert did not like his father marrying Eliza,' she said.

'Why did he object so much? The other children all appear to get along with her fine.'

'Robert's conventional. He has a picture in his head of what things ought to be like, and he gets upset when reality doesn't agree. Takes after his mother in that respect, if Ursula is to believed.'

'You're probably right. Anyway, I think we need the perspective of someone who wasn't in the house last weekend. I'm going to talk to Farndale's old business partner,' Collins said.

'Victor hadn't been working for years, surely you don't think this was a business matter which has been simmering for all that time?'

'No, but I want to hear about him from someone who wasn't competing for his attention. His children are all incapable of seeing him except in relation to themselves.'

'Good point. Was there anything interesting in Simon Danvers's journal?'

'If Jake wants to be a writer I really hope he has inherited more of his mother's talent than Simon has.'

'Anything useful?' Sally amended.

'Unless this is a very clever fiction – of which I do not believe Simon Danvers capable – he has nothing to do with it.'

'Is he short of money?'

'Not exactly. He has his inheritance from his grandfather and he does some freelance work. There's money coming in, but according to Jake he's not very good at keeping hold of it.'

'And having a girlfriend who wants to be treated to lunch at the Radetzki at least once a week is not helping,' she concluded.

'Exactly. Still, it's a weak motive, and I don't think that Simon is that devious. More the type who does what he's told.'

He was the exact opposite of his brother in that respect.

DI Graham had been right, it was just a question of waiting for the next incident. Despite the extra constables on patrol around the Newmarket, another attack happened that night.

Peter brought them up to speed during the CID meeting on Friday. 'The victim is called Ben Dutton, twenty-five years old, and he was set upon at 2:30 by five black-clad assailants.'

'*Five* assailants? I thought there were only four in the other cases?'

'There were, but Dutton is adamant there were five coming at him. He does – what's it called? – aikido, he put up quite a fight, and I think his situational awareness is much better than that of the earlier victims. But there's more. The bouncer at Bitters saw a young guy run away from Walker Alley just before uniform arrived and recognised him. I just hope it isn't just the bouncer trying to drop someone in it.'

'Who was it?'

'The guy he saw is called Tyler Whitaker – nothing known. The man who called it in was Barry Andrews.'

'Oh, Bazza's all right. If he bothered to call us you can trust it is serious.'

'Good. Josh and Pardoe can pick him up straight after the meeting.'

Two hours later they had Tyler Whitaker in an interview room. Graham asked Collins to sit in, since Josh had been up since the call came in at three o'clock and was threatening to fall asleep where he sat.

'You are Tyler Adam Whitaker, born February 15 1997?'

A grudging nod.

'Please speak up for the recording.'

'Yeah, I'm Tyler Whitaker.'

'Any relation to Gail Whitaker over at Five Willows Farm?' Collins asked.

A flicker of surprise this time. 'She's my auntie.'

'Right,' Graham took over, 'We have a witness who saw you last night, at around half past two, running away from Walker Alley. Care to tell us why?'

'I wasn't doing anything wrong.'

'That's not really an answer to my question, is it? Why were you in such a hurry to get away, Tyler?'

Whitaker continued to look sullenly at the table between them. 'I had nothing to do with it, okay?'

Graham tried a sterner approach.

'Mr Whitaker, can you tell me what you were doing in Walker Alley tonight, and why you were in such a hurry to get away from there?'

'Look, I'd nothing to do with it!' the boy repeated, 'I just saw all the coppers and panicked.'

'And why should the police cause you to panic, Mr Whitaker?'

'Doesn't matter, does it? I swear I didn't beat up that guy.'

Collins was reminded of the first time he had ever spoken to Jake, although that had been in the back of a pub, not an interview room. He had looked at him with that same moodily defiant gaze from under his fringe, had spoken with the same nervous bravado of a boy who knew he was in trouble, testing him, trying to find out how much he could get away with. There were obvious differences as well, of course. Dark gold skin where Jake was pale, deep brown eyes instead of blue, sulky half-sentences where Jake was never lost for words. And with Jake there had also been a different, more furtive assessment going on. He doubted he and this boy would be cosily having tea at Costa in a few weeks' time. Tyler Whitaker clearly wanted nothing but to be out of here as quickly as possible. And that wish was soon to be granted, because apart from being seen fleeing by Bazza, there really was nothing to tie the boy to the attack on Ben Dutton.

In the CID room, there were photos of the victims up on the whiteboard. A smarmy studio portrait for Murray, a fuzzy holiday snap for Khan, an action shot from the gym for

Briggs, and a tousle-haired, crinkle-eyed selfie for Dutton. The four men really did not have anything in common.

'Ben Dutton's gay. So, queer-bashing?' Rowena suggested.

'I think that's just coincidence,' Collins said, 'Thursday is gay night at Bitters, after all.'

DC Robbins, back after a few hours sleep, opened his mouth for the first time. 'They have a gay night at Bitters? I've never seen it advertised.'

'They never advertised, it just sort of happened.'

Josh fell silent again, apparently trying to recall whether he had recently spent a Thursday night clubbing, and whether to be relieved or insulted that he hadn't noticed.

DCI Dixon ignored the by-play. 'It's the only thing approximating a reason we've got.'

'But the others are all straight,' Pardoe protested.

'Maybe there was something else wrong with them,' DCI Dixon said, and then added hastily, 'In the eyes of the attackers, I mean.'

'Oh yes, a spot of victim-blaming, I knew I was missing something,' DS Holmes said when Collins repeated the conversation to her later.

'Sally, be serious. However badly she puts it, Rowena has a point. The only thing the victims have in common is that they are young, or youngish, males. And they don't pick on the weakest, either. Conor Briggs spends all his spare time in the gym, and Ben Dutton does aikido.'

Sally pushed her hair out of her eyes. 'I know, I know, it is just that she rubs me the wrong way. I was ribbing Josh about something yesterday – I don't even remember what – and she became all uppity about making sure that younger officers feel welcome in the team. I mean, what's the point of a detective who can't tell the difference between banter and bullying?'

'Oh, so that's why! I had a very strange talk with her this morning, actually,' Josh said, coming in behind them, 'She wanted to know if I was all right, and if there was anything I 'wanted to share' with her.' He made quotes in the air with his fingers. 'She said sometimes when a new member joins a team, the old hands join ranks, and it can be very difficult to win their trust, and she wanted to be sure I would let her know if I ever felt excluded.' He shook his head. 'I've been here for five months! Like I wouldn't have said something before now.'

'That, son, is what the psychologists call projection,' Pardoe said.

'*Are* we closing ranks against her?' Collins asked Sally.

'Not that I'm aware, but if she carries on like this we will. Are you off to Farndale Tech, then?'

25

'I thought it was just a random attack, surely there is nothing I can tell you?'

Collins looked at Mr Mitchell and tried to make sense of his words. There really was no way Victor Farndale's murder could be described as a random attack. 'I'm sorry?'

'One of our employees was attacked last night, I thought that was what you were here about.'

'Oh, Ben Dutton works here?'

'One of our most talented game developers. But you're not here about that apparently.'

'No, my colleagues are on that case, interviewing witnesses as we speak. I am here to talk to you about Victor Farndale.'

'Of course, I'm sorry. Crossed lines there. What do you want to know?'

What he mostly wanted to know was if Victor had had enemies, and if Colin Mitchell was one of them. But he couldn't detect any animosity or lingering resentment in the way the man spoke about his late business partner.

'We parted ways in business, but not socially,' Mitchell explained, 'My children, Scott and Natasha, 'hang out', as I believe they call it, with Mortimer, Victor's son, they've all known each other since they were little. They were all here last night, as a matter of fact.'

He was aware of that connection already, of course. Collins tried another tack.

'I understand that when Victor retired the company moved out of Ulvercott House. Could you not have continued there? The house is large enough.'

'Victor would not have objected, but with the new building in Abbey Hill finished it wasn't necessary. There is not such a need to have people working on site these days. Of course in the creative divisions it is important to get people into one room and talking, like the game designers do here, but we encourage the coders and the accountants and such people to work from home whenever possible, and save on travel.'

And save on other things, no doubt. Or was he being cynical? Possibly it was simply that a virtuous desire to lower carbon emissions coincided happily with cutting down on office space and free coffee. But at least Farndale Tech still had an office in the neighbourhood. One of Victor's most popular policies had been to employ local people whenever possible. If you called the Farndale Tech helpdesk you wouldn't be talking to someone halfway across the world. He wondered if Mitchell still kept that up. He had already given his visitor a spiel about 'streamlining' the company since he had taken over, and how he was steering a different course from his predecessor.

'Victor was a great businessman, a great businessman. But he was of another generation, you know what I mean? Employees these days don't thrive on that paternalistic attitude. They want to feel as if they are all equal contributors to the communal effort.'

With 'as if' being the operative term, he supposed. Collins reacted to business-speak in much the same way Sally did to inherited wealth, and he had to keep reminding himself that professing a *commitment to transparent communication strategies* didn't automatically make someone a crook.

Paternalistic or not, he had the feeling he would have preferred talking to Victor Farndale rather than to his business partner. And Mitchell hadn't even told him anything useful.

At the station, he found Sally poring over the timeline Nora Farndale had made for them.

'Don't you know that by heart by now?'

'Yeah, but I wasn't looking at what it says, more how it says it, if you know what I mean.'

'Go on.'

'Well, don't you think this is all rather cold? *Apart from Victor's unexpected death, there was nothing unusual about the weekend's events,*' she read, 'It's as if she is deliberately distancing herself from what happened.'

'Perhaps. Or perhaps it is just her way of making sense of things.'

Sally gave him a look. 'Sometimes I wonder how you ever made it to inspector. You would give everyone the benefit of the doubt if you could.'

'Well, if you want proof that I am just as prejudiced as anyone else, I didn't like Colin Mitchell at all. Or that Swift bloke Mortimer hangs out with.'

'Anything useful from Mitchell?'

'Nothing really.'

They were both silent for a bit.

'We're stuck, aren't we?' Sally said at length.

'Pretty much.'

'So what are you going to tell Rowena?'

'That we have eliminated a number of people from our inquiries, and that we are confident of making more progress going forward.'

'Nice one.'

On Sunday, as Dominic had said, they had Jake and Noah over for dinner. It was the first time Collins had properly met Jake's boyfriend, and, not for the first time, he wondered how on earth they had managed to get together. Noah Rosenthal might look like he had escaped from a boyband, but he hardly spoke at all, and when he did it was to Dominic, who was his supervisor at uni. That did give Owen the opportunity of catching up with Jake, though.

'Are you in touch with your brother Simon at all?'

'Not really. Mum set up this family WhatsApp group, but only me and Rachel ever reply to her messages. Why, what's he done?'

'Nothing, I think, which makes a change. But his girlfriend's father has died in suspicious circumstances.'

'Of course,' Jake said, with a weariness which would have suited someone forty years older, 'Trust Simon to jump out of the frying pan into the fire. You sure he had nothing to do with it?'

In anyone else that would have been a very cynical question, but Owen had a history with Jake's family.

'I would be very surprised if he had. Have you actually met his girlfriend?'

'No, I've only heard about her. What's she called again? Something Greek – Hermione?'

'Antigone.'

'That's it. Is she in the frame?'

'You know I can't answer that.'

Owen knew officers who never talked about their cases at home, who left police work in the office and didn't breathe a word to their loved ones. He really didn't understand how they did it. He knew he had to change the subject, but that only led to him speaking of another case.

'Jake, do you still go to Bitters on Thursdays?'

'Not so often these days. Is this you warning me about the Butcher's Row gang? I heard Ben Dutton got attacked.'

'Do you know him?'

'Not to speak to. Just as someone who also goes to Bitters. Don't worry, Owen, I won't go wandering around town on my own until you've caught them. Anyway, I haven't yet managed to persuade Noah to go to the club.'

'I don't like crowds,' Noah offered.

'And you think half a dozen people is a crowd,' Jake said with a grin. 'Never mind, I'd rather keep you to myself anyway.'

Dominic gave Owen a look which said, as plainly as if he had spoken: 'See? They're all right, those two'.

26

Eden

From: evkingston@umail.co.uk
To: owen.collins@mailspace.com
Re: Ulvercott

Dear Mr Collins,

I got your email address from Jake, I'm sorry, I should probably just have called the police station, but I don't know if this is really important, and since you said to let you know if I thought of anything... here I am.

When I was clearing out the attic with Jacqueline and Mrs Farndale the weekend of the 25th, I found an old envelope tucked away on top of one of the beams, where it met the slope of the roof. It looked like a kid's hiding place to me. The envelope – a package really, there was more than just a letter in it – was addressed to 'Annabel and Victor', and it was still sealed. Since it was for him and his wife, instead of putting it with the other papers we found I gave it to Mr Farndale before I left. I thought it must be very strange to receive a letter which had been lying there unopened for what could be twenty years... But later, when they said Mr Farndale had been murdered, I thought what if he had learned something dangerous, something the killer wanted to stay hidden? I don't know what happened to the letter after I gave it to Mr

Farndale, and neither does Jacqueline. I may be imagining things, but at least I've told you now.

Kind regards,

Eden Kingston

27

Since the fourth attack in the town centre the media had become even more scathing about the failure of the police to apprehend the culprits, and so Rowena Dixon decided to take the offensive. She outlined her plan for trapping the Butcher's Row gang in the CID meeting on Monday morning. All plainclothes officers under forty were to patrol the area on Thursday night, mingling with the crowd, trying to identify trouble before it was too late.

'That's going to cost a lot of money,' was DI Graham's first comment.

'I know, but it will be worth it,' Rowena enthused, 'The gang know the uniformed constables who patrol there by sight, it wouldn't be any use to put them in civilian clothes. But they are unlikely to recognise you lot.'

'Unless Tyler Whitaker really is one of them.'

'But you let him go.'

'Lack of evidence, not lack of suspicion, I assure you,' Graham said, 'But then I won't be out in the field, so to speak. I assume you want me to coordinate?'

'Yes, with Pardoe. Robbins, Holmes and Collins will be out in the field, as you call it. Behave as if you are going out for the night, dress up – that means heels, and more cleavage, Sally – don't let anyone suspect you are working. The gang will be out there, watching for an opportunity, and we will be watching them.'

'What, just the three of us?'

'I'm sure I can rustle up a couple more bodies from Oxford,' DCI Dixon said.

The logical thing to do would have been to draw in uniformed constables from other stations for the entire operation, but Collins thought he understood why she was reluctant to do that. She wanted the credit to go to her own team if the op was successful.

'Sally? You still with us?' Collins asked, when Rowena had left.

'Ye-es. I was just wondering whether your female and presumably straight boss telling you to show more cleavage is actually sexist.'

'She certainly has a knack for choosing the wrong words,' Collins said.

'Is that all it is, though? I don't mean about the cleavage remark, that's just funny. But are we sure that this,' she waved her arms about, 'This whole operation is a good idea?'

It had been bothering him as well. It all smelled like a new broom trying to enter with a splash (and that really was a terribly mixed metaphor). There wasn't enough time to prepare an op this size, but Rowena wouldn't hear of postponing it until next week.

'We can't wait until there's been another attack, the public are getting impatient, they're asking what we're doing,' she had said.

The public were always asking what they were doing, at the same time as looking forward eagerly to the next sensational headline. It shouldn't be a consideration, really, but they all felt the pressure.

'It can't do any harm,' he told Sally, although he didn't sound very convincing even to himself. They'd just have to follow orders and see what happened. Meanwhile, they had their own case to get on with. He told the sergeant about Eden Kingston's email.

'SOCO didn't find anything like that, did they?'

'No, which raises the possibility that it was important, and someone got rid of it. I've asked Eden to meet me at Ulvercott today, show me where she found the letter. You can ask Ursula if she knows anything about it.'

'But what if Ursula is the one who got rid of the letter in the first place?'

'That's a risk we'll have to run. We'll never get a warrant for a full-scale search with the case we've got right now. And of all of them, I think Ursula is the least likely to be reading other people's correspondence.'

'That's a point.'

He found Eden Kingston in the kitchen at Ulvercott, having coffee with Oliver Farndale. He hadn't figured Oliver for the type to mix with the servants, but they looked very relaxed and friendly together. Did Eden have another reason besides psychological interest for returning to work at Ulvercott House?

'Oh, Inspector, you've come about the package, I suppose?'

Oliver hurriedly got up. 'You're here on business, I'd better go. See you, Eden.'

The last time Collins had seen her, Eden's hair had been in neat cornrows. This time she sported a head of loose, glossy black curls with golden highlights.

'I realise that 'what happened to you hair?' may not be the most gallant way to put it but—'

She grinned. 'But what happened to my hair? Basically, my cousin is a trainee hairdresser and I'm a guinea pig. It means I get free treatments, but sometimes they're not what I would have chosen myself.' She fingered a curl. 'This isn't all my own, obviously. Extensions. Shall we go up to the attic?'

Having become a proud home-owner recently, Collin realised that when Eden said 'attic', he had been thinking about the light space under the roof he and Dominic had turned into the study. This was something else entirely. The attic ran the entire length of the east wing, with creaking floorboards and massive wooden crossbeams. It was as cold here as it was outside, and there were frost patterns on the windows. He couldn't recall when he'd last seen those.

'Me and Jacqueline worked with coats and gloves on,' Eden said, 'And lots of coffee breaks.'

'Why now, though? Couldn't it have waited till the spring?'

'There's a firm coming to do roof repairs in March. They wanted the attic cleared out before then.'

'I see. And where did you found the envelope?'

She pointed to a joist. 'I'm not tall enough to have spotted it from here, but I was on the stepladder trying to get the blinds off that window.'

'It must have been there for years.'

'There was a thick layer of dust on it. I'm afraid I can't say anything about footsteps,' she said, only half joking, 'Jacqueline brought the hoover up here. Anyway, I took the envelope down and saw the names on it, so I gave it to Mr Farndale. I can't be sure, of course, but it looked as if it hadn't been opened.'

Neither Ursula nor Jacqueline could tell Sally what had happened to the package Eden had found, and she was in the hallway of Ulvercott wondering whether questioning the whole family once again or applying for a search warrant was the more expensive and time-consuming, when Matt walked in.

'Matt, how are you?' she said, as casually as she could.

'Hi, Sal. I'm fine, although I do feel as if I'm here under false pretences.'

'That's because you are. But you do want to find out who killed Victor, don't you? You liked him.' Somehow, it was very important to establish that he wasn't here for Electra.

'Yes, but I can't say I've learned anything useful from the other members of the family. There's one thing, though...'

'Yes?'

'When Robert went to lock his father's rooms on Saturday, he was away too long. He went into Victor's rooms before locking them, and after that he went somewhere else – his own bedroom, I assume – before returning to the others. I know because I went to help Jacqueline in the kitchen, and we could hear him moving about upstairs. All the others were in the sitting room. It may just be that Robert wanted a moment to himself, his father had just died, after all. That, or—'

Or there was something in Victor's room he didn't want anyone else to find, Sally concluded. 'Thanks Matt, you've no idea how helpful that is. I have to tell my boss right away.'

She found Collins in the incident room uploading photos of the attic onto the system. There was a black cat sitting on the desk next to him, scrutinising the progress bar.

'It was Robert,' she said, 'It was Robert who took the package away, I'm sure if it.'

She rapidly told him what she had learned from Matt.

'You're probably right. But I don't see how a twenty-year old letter, or whatever it is, can be incriminating to Robert now.'

'We'll understand when we know what's in it. Ursula and Jacqueline know nothing about it, but I haven't asked Eliza yet. Victor may have told her what was in the envelope, after all.'

'No, he didn't tell me, Sergeant' Eliza said, 'This is the first I've heard of it. But I think I can help you anyway. If there was a letter, Victor would certainly have scanned it. He digitised everything before most people even knew what the word meant. If it was important he would have made sure there was a copy. I know the password to his computer – shall I have a look?'

There was only one new document dated a few days before Victor's death, and it was a scan of a handwritten letter.

'Maite?' Eliza said wonderingly. 'I've never heard that name.'

But Sally had. It was in Ursula Westmacott's statement. Maite de Burgos was the Farndales' Spanish au pair girl when the twins were babies. And before she left she had written a letter to her employers which had lain in the attic for twenty-eight years before being delivered.

28

Maite

Letter from Maite de Burgos to Victor and Annabel Farndale, dated January 1987

Dear Victor and Annabel,

I am sorry for burdening you with this, but I believe it is the best thing to do.
His name is Mateo. You know whose child he is.
I told you I was going back to Spain, and that is true, but I haven't gone yet. I told no one when I found out I was pregnant, I wanted time to myself to figure out what to do. I thought England might be a better place to be an unmarried mother than Spain. But I didn't get the time to figure things out, because of what the doctors found during the prenatal check-up.
I have an aggressive form of cancer. I may have months to live, or only weeks. So now I am going back to Spain, to be with my family in my last days. I do not know what they would say if I brought my son with me. They are good Catholics and I do not want Mateo's life to begin in guilt and recrimination. And his father should have a say, even if right now he may not want anything to do with this. I would like Mateo to grow up with your family, with your little girls as sisters, in the place where you have always made me feel welcome. I know you will not fail me, or him. I have left a

message for him also, for when he is old enough to hear it. I'll leave it to you to decide when that is.
Thank you for all you have done, and all you will do, with all my heart.

Maria Teresa de Burgos González

29

DS Holmes was furious, and Collins didn't know what to do. Sally didn't have a good word to say about Victor Farndale now, and she was not going about it quietly.

'All of them talking about what a family man he was, all of them so fond of 'dad'. But when he had a child with the au pair St Bride's was good enough. It makes me sick!'

'Sally!'

'Don't try to defend him, all right? Dumping your own child in the care system so you won't have to ruin the pretty picture? I'm glad someone killed him. He deserved it!'

She walked away from him, muttering something that sounded like 'two-faced chauvinist wanker'.

He hurried after her. 'Sally, come back. Victor Farndale was not the father of Maite's child!'

She stopper in her tracks. 'Wait, what? But the letter...'

'It is addressed to both Victor and Annabel, and says 'you know whose child he is'. It doesn't name Victor as the father.'

'Oh.'

'Sally, think about all we have learned about Victor, the man who wanted to have a family so much that he did it three times. Would he have left a child of his to be raised in St Bride's of all places? And why are you so sure the child went to St Bride's anyway?'

She frowned. 'Whose child was he then?'

'Robert's, I would guess. That would explain why he hid the letter. It was probably him that hid it in the attic in the first place.'

'But he was only a child himself,' she protested.

'No. Remember there was quite a gap between him and Electra and Antigone. Robert was in his late teens when Maite arrived to look after the twins.'

'So what do *you* think happened?'

'Look, I'll tell you, but can we please talk about this somewhere else than in full view of the house?'

'Yeah, sorry. I was just so angry.'

'And with reason. But not at Victor.'

They went back inside, to their incident room. Sally still looked almost feral.

'A baby born in December 1986. A baby called Mateo,' she muttered.

Only then did it click. That was why this upset Sally so much. That was why she immediately thought of St Bride's. Maite's baby would be twenty-eight now. Maite's baby could be Matt Fielding.

'I never thought. How did Matt end up at St Bride? Aren't there records?'

'No, he told you, remember? He was a foundling. It still happens sometimes, you know. He was left in the yard at St Bride's when he was about a month old. They couldn't trace his mother.'

'So he could be Maite's child,' Owen said, 'But then, what went wrong? The letter clearly states that she intended him to go to Victor and Annabel, but there's no indication that Victor even knew of his existence.'

He was glad to see that Sally looked a little calmer now. 'Victor only got the letter a few weeks ago, he can't have known,' she said.

'It would have been risky though, if she planned to spring it on them like that. But what if Maite had already told Robert? What if she believed they already knew about the child? She comes across as a sensible girl, don't you think? Especially considering she had to contend with an unplanned pregnancy and illness in a foreign country. Surely she would have told the child's father she was expecting?'

'But then why did it go wrong?'

'At a guess, because Robert did what boys that age do with all their problems: ignore it and hope it goes away. He certainly wouldn't have told his father.'

Sally frowned. 'That still doesn't explain why Matt didn't go to Victor and Annabel. But wait– what if Maite died suddenly, and had no time to do as she planned?'

'Surely the child wouldn't have ended up on the doorstep of St Bride's in that case? Social services would have traced the next of kin, and the baby would have ended up with the Farndales anyway.'

'Yes, you're right, that doesn't wash.'

'I think Maite went to Ulvercott, and found Robert at home alone, so she gave him the child and the letter. After all, he was the father, and she trusted him to explain the situation to Victor and his stepmother,' Collins said.

'But he didn't, he just got rid of the baby, and Victor didn't learn about its existence until just before he died. What a bastard. Robert, I mean. Do you think the relationship was consensual?'

'It must have been. I don't think Maite would have wanted her baby to live with Robert's family otherwise. And there's no bitterness about her pregnancy in the letter. Just sadness about having to leave her child.'

He looked at the document again. 'She says she left a message for the child. There must have been a tape in the envelope. Eden is sure there was something more substantial in the package.'

'I just hope he hasn't destroyed it this time around. Matt needs to hear that tape. Oh God, how do we tell him this?'

'We don't tell him at all yet. No, really Sally, we don't. Remember we don't know for certain that he is Maite's baby.'

'Yeah, right.'

He looked at her. 'Evidence, DS Holmes. No case without evidence.'

'All right, all right. Let's go back to the station and find some.'

'There is no death for a Maria Teresa de Burgos registered in the UK in 1986-87,' Josh Robbins said, fingers flying over the keyboard, 'But there is a birth certificate for a Mateo de Burgos in 1986.'

'Thanks, Josh. Facts, that's what we need.'

'So she must have gone back to Spain as planned,' Sally said.

'But she won't be around anymore to ask. One thing is certain, Robert Farndale has some explaining to do.'

'Shall we bring him in?'

'Hold your horses. I want to make sure we've got the facts straight. It could be that Victor told someone what he had learned, and that was why he was murdered. Perhaps that was why his solicitor was there on Friday. Let's first find out all we can about this business, and *then* we bring in Robert Farndale. You'd better ring Taylor, Weir and Taylor again. And Josh, see if you can track down Maite's GP or oncologist. They may well remember what happened to her and the child. It could still be coincidence, and have nothing to do with Mr Fielding.'

Not that he believed that himself, of course.

'Do you have anything planned on Thursday night?' Owen asked Dominic when he got home, head still reeling from the day's revelations.

'Nothing special. Are you on late shift?'

'Night shift, in fact.'

Dominic raised his eyebrows. 'Trying to catch the Butcher's Row gang in flagrante?'

'Not supposed to tell.'

'I'll count that as a yes.'

Owen looked at him. 'It doesn't upset you at all, does it? That I need to work at night at short notice.'

'Should it?' Dominic asked. 'You know, in books and on TV the detectives' partners are always complaining about their working hours, and I keep thinking 'you knew that when you married him'. I mean, you wouldn't be you if you didn't care about your job, and then I wouldn't care so much about you.'

'I think that sentence needs a little work, but I see what you mean.'

'Anyway, the new bookcases will be delivered on Thursday afternoon. Any chance you can be at home for that?'

'Yes, actually. If I'm working at night I can take some time off earlier.'

30

'I did not kill my father. In the event that you got it into your heads that I had. I didn't want to this ever to get out, but I prefer it to being tried for murder.'

Robert Farndale was being interviewed, and it hadn't taken long to establish that what had taken place twenty-eight years ago was much as they had conjectured. Robert's solicitor appeared to agree that not getting charged with murder was paramount, and let his client talk freely.

'We are by no means convinced that you did not murder your father, Mr Farndale. After all he was going to reveal your big secret, wasn't he? He had already spoken with Mr Taylor about the necessary steps for identifying Matt as his grandson.'

'He had? I did not know that.'

'Don't lie, Mr Farndale.'

'It's the truth! I just noticed the package in my father's room when I went in there after he died.'

'And decided to take it.'

'Yes.'

'What else was in there apart from the letter?'

Farndale reached into his inside pocket. 'This.'

It was a cassette tape with 'For Mateo' written on it in black marker.

Collins was beginning to feel almost as angry as Sally. This man had found a message for his son from the boy's dead mother among his own recently deceased father's things, and his only thought had been what the consequences for himself would be. An eighteen-year-old boy literally left holding the baby could, at a stretch, be forgiven for not considering the impact of his actions on the lives of others. In a man in his forties, with a wife and children, it was contemptible.

'Right, that is child abandonment, theft, withholding evidence...'

The solicitor cleared his throat and spoke for the first time. 'Child abandonment? I really don't think...'

'You must be aware that it is a criminal offence for a parent not to take care of their child. Your client can look forward to a lengthy prison sentence.'

'A *parent*?'

Sally looked at Robert Farndale's indignant expression and realised that he had never thought of himself as the child's father until now. He had always thought of Matt as Maite's baby. He really hadn't considered himself responsible. She had thought that his wish to hide the evidence stemmed from a sense of guilt, but she had been wrong. He was just trying to save his reputation.

'You don't care, do you?' she asked him, even though Collins was leading on this one, 'About Maite, about the child, not even about Victor. *He* would have cared, but you'd rather keep his good opinion than give your child a place to live.'

'Now look here, young lady—'

'Don't you 'young lady' me! You denied a dying woman's wish and your child a loving home, and you're sitting there being self-righteous about it. You're despicable.'

Sally got up, knowing that she had already gone too far, knowing she had to get out.

'This is outrageous!' Robert protested, 'I want to talk to the person in charge here.'

'Then talk to the bitch in the heels! I'm done.'

She slammed the door of the interview room behind her and ran upstairs.

'Sally! Come back down here this instant!'

Rowena, she thought, as she sat in her desk chair, folding herself around the sobs that seemed to force their way out from somewhere deep in her stomach, Rowena had been observing the interview. She had heard that. All of it. Sally pressed a balled tissue to her mouth. Oh my God, I lost my rag with a suspect and insulted my boss into the bargain. And I'd do it again, I'd do it again.

'Sally?'

DCI Dixon appeared in the doorway, looking apprehensive behind the hipster glasses. 'What happened?'

She was all kindness now. Sally couldn't tell if it was real or just what Rowena thought was the appropriate response in the circumstances. But here Sally herself was on firmer ground. She had a lot of experience with authority figures speaking more in sorrow than in anger. Time to play for sympathy.

'I'm sorry, ma'am. I shouldn't have let rip like that, but Farndale hit a nerve. Have you got children?'

'No. I'm a career girl, me.'

She closed her eyes. Christ, but she disliked Rowena Dixon. Concentrate, Sally. Sympathy, remember?

'Imagine you had a baby, though, and you didn't have long to live. You think you have found a good home for your child. And then the father decides he doesn't want to own up, and he puts the kid on the doorstep of a children's home instead. Twenty-eight years of not knowing why. Twenty-eight years of not knowing who you are. Because some spoiled rich kid didn't want his own childhood to end. I couldn't just sit there, with him still thinking he could get away with it. With him thinking it didn't matter. It matters. It matters *so* much.'

Real tears now. And somehow this was worst of all. To show her true emotions to a woman she did not like, and did not trust, but whose decision right now could make or break the career of Detective Sergeant Holmes.

'I understand this is difficult for you, Sally. DI Collins should never have allowed you to conduct the interview.'

Oh God, she couldn't blame Collie?

'It was me who insisted on staying on the case, ma'am.'

'But we all know that sometimes we shouldn't take those decisions ourselves, don't we? You are not seeing things clearly right now. That's perfectly understandable. But we should not allow that to influence the progress of the investigation. I shall speak to DI Collins about your personal involvement in this case.'

'It is only this part of the investigation which touches me personally, ma'am. I can continue with the murder inquiry.'

DCI Dixon looked surprised. 'But— Do you mean to say that Robert Farndale did *not* kill his father?'

'Well, I don't know what he has said since I, er, left the interview room, of course, but I'd say there is a fair chance that Robert is not the killer.'

'Then what have we got him in for?'

So much for sympathy.

'Child abandonment?'

'Oh, yes, of course. I'm a bit off kilter myself. Sorry.'

It looked like she didn't know what to say next. Sally couldn't wait for her to get out of the room, but there was still the little matter of what she had shouted at Robert Farndale as she ran from the interview room. Rowena must have heard that too, but she didn't say anything about it.

And then Sally realised: the DCI did not know what to do. If she acknowledged that she had heard what Sally had called her she would have to take action, and that would probably result in an internal inquiry, with one or both of them – be honest, probably just Sally – being suspended for the duration. And Rowena, who had been complaining about the small size of her team from day one, didn't want to be an officer short for her big operation. If she pretended not to have heard they could carry on just as before, and no one would be questioning DCI Dixon's conduct either. So all she would have to do was copy her boss and act like it had never happened.

'With your permission, ma'am, I'd like to take the rest of the day off. I need to get myself together.'

'Of course, of course. Take as long as you like,' DCI Dixon said, sounding rather relieved.

'Detective Sergeant Holmes has left the room,' Collins said, for the recording. 'DI Peter Graham enters. Peter, can you take over from DS Holmes? She is, er, indisposed.'

'Of course.'

Robert Farndale looked from one detective to the other. '*Indisposed?* She insulted me! This is police harassment. Aren't you going to do anything about it?'

'Ah, well,' Peter said, taking Sally's seat. 'I know modern police practice requires officers to remain dispassionate. But me, I'm an old-fashioned man. I see a young woman, one who wants to have children of her own one day maybe, imagining what it is like to have to trust your baby to someone else,' he leant forward, '*And then have that trust betrayed.* Don't even think about complaining, Mr Farndale. Be glad she only shouted at you.'

Remarkably, Mr Farndale's solicitor had remained silent throughout all this. He appeared to have decided that if his client wanted to dig holes for himself, there was nothing he could do about it.

They spent the rest of the interview establishing the exact sequence of events, and reluctantly admitting to themselves that there was no indication that Robert had killed Victor.

'Defence will argue that he panicked and was too young to be held responsible for what he did to Matt,' Graham said after the uniformed constable had taken Farndale back to his cell.

'Possibly. Prosecution will have a field day with his attempts to conceal his crime, though. It's practically an admission of guilt.'

'True. I doubt any of it will make as much of an impression as our Sally, though. Did she really call Rowena...?'

'The bitch in the heels? 'Fraid so. Thanks for stepping in there, by the way. I'd better go and see her now. Sally, I mean. I'm not sure I can handle the DCI after two hours of Robert Farndale.'

But Graham held him back. 'No, wait a moment. What do I need to know about Sally?'

'She grew up in St Bride's herself.'

'I see. And she's, what, three years younger than Mr Fielding?'

'Exactly. From what I hear St Bride's in the nineties wasn't a bad place to grow up. But Mr Robert Farndale did not know that when he dumped his own child there, did he?'

'You shouldn't have let her interview him.'

'Maybe not. But then, I really don't think that we are here to protect Mr Farndale from the consequences of his actions.'

'Then for her own sake?' Graham suggested.

'I don't think Sally would have appreciated my coming over all protective, and she would have had to confront it at some point. I have to admit I hadn't counted on her throwing in a dig at DCI Dixon.'

'Yes, that was unfortunate,' DI Graham said drily, 'And I have no idea which way *she* will jump.'

'Me neither.'

Christ, he hoped Dixon wouldn't suspend Sally, he needed her on the job. They might have a case against Robert Farndale now, but the murder investigation was still no further forward.

'I'll talk to her. Try to soften things a bit,' Graham offered.

'Thanks.'

Sally was nowhere to be found, so he sent her a text to ask if she was all right, and then dropped by the tech department on his way.

'Meg, can you play commercial cassette tapes on our old interview recorders? Is that the same format?'

'I'm an IT specialist, Owen, and cassette tapes where on the way out before I was born. I've no idea. You'll just have to try.'

He got one of the old tape machines from the cellar and inserted the cassette. That looked all right. He pressed play. After more than twenty years in a cold attic, the sound quality wasn't great, but even if it had been, it would have been little use to him. There was only a woman's voice, presumably Maite's, speaking in Spanish. He didn't know why he hadn't thought about that before. He went back to the CID room.

'Josh, find me an accredited Spanish interpreter, will you?'

'Will do, sir. Oh and speaking of Spain, I've been in touch with the Guardia Civil. Maite de Burgos returned to Spain in January 1987, and died at her parents' house in Pradillo two weeks later. Do you want someone to talk to the family?'

'Let's not worry them until we know what's what. They probably have no idea that Maite ever had a child.'

31

Maite

Transcription of cassette tape found at Ulvercott House, translation by P. Sánchez Lang

My name is Maria Teresa de Burgos González. They call me Maite. It is January 1987 and I'm making this tape for you, Mateo, so you will understand why I cannot be there to talk to you in person. Your grandparents will give you this tape when they think you are old enough.
I came to England a year and a half ago to work as an au pair for Victor and Annabel Farndale, looking after their twin girls. Victor also had a son from his first marriage, Robert. He was seventeen at the time, and very good-looking. I was nineteen, and feeling lonely in a strange country. By the time you hear this, you will be old enough to understand what that means.
I was already pregnant when I learned that I was seriously ill. Fatally ill. They gave me a year, at best, possibly less. I knew before you were born that I would not see you grow up. I had to think about who would look after you.
I felt surprisingly well all through my pregnancy, but the dizzy spells are getting more frequent now, and I am exhausted. You are only a month old, and I know I don't have long. Nobody knows about you yet apart from the doctors and nurses, but I've made arrangements. You will have a good home. Your father is too young to raise a child of his own, but I know your grandparents will take care of you and love

you as you should be loved. I am so sorry that I must leave you alone my darling, but I imagine you all grown up in that big house, and then things aren't so bad.

[Sound of a baby crying and Maite singing *'Duermete mi niño'*.]

I am very tired now, and I know I must let you go soon. I have done everything I had to. The letter is written. I have your carrycot ready, with a supply of formula and nappies. I have tucked your little fox in with you. As soon as you are asleep we will go.

[pause]

I don't want to do this, but I have to. What if I collapse and don't come to again? Who would take care of you then?

I'm sorry, I didn't mean to burden you with that. I'll take you to your family now, my Mateo. I hope you will be very happy. I know I will be proud of you, wherever I am.

Te quiero cielo. Para siempre.

32

Sally returned to work the next morning as if nothing had happened, and no one referred to the incident in the interview room. Robert Farndale had been released on bail after handing over the tape and making a full statement, and instead of on the Farndale case, the CID meeting was spent on planning tomorrow's attempt to catch the Butcher's Row gang. Collins found it hard to concentrate though. His thoughts kept returning to Maite's last message.

The gang had apparently been random in the timing of the attacks, so there was no guarantee that they would be abroad on Thursday night. He wondered if Rowena had considered the scenario in which the press learned that the Butcher's Row gang had attacked their next victim the night *after* the police had gone after them mob-handed. Because the press would learn of the op. There would be a uniform with a mate at the Messenger, or a girlfriend who worked for local television. They might keep quiet until Thursday night, but the cat would be let out of the bag afterwards. And if they ended up empty- as well as mob-handed, well, there would still be headlines.

'Why Thursday?' he asked, trying to show willing.

'The attacks until now happened once a week, once on Friday and Saturday, and twice on a Thursday. We can never be sure, but it seems the best bet.'

'Yes, I agree, but what I meant is, isn't that a bit short notice? Do we have time to get all safeguards in place? And doesn't the Chief Super have to okay this?'

'There is no need for you to worry about that. And we have to act now.'

'What I don't understand is why you want senior CID officers on this operation? Wouldn't it be more practical to employ uniformed constables in plain clothes?' Graham said.

'Not to mention cheaper,' Sally put in. 'Not that I mind about the overtime.'

'Most of the uniformed constables have patrolled the town centre at one time or another. The gang will almost certainly be familiar with their faces.'

That made sense, although he was surprised that DCI Dixon had got it past her superiors.

'I've managed to borrow two uniformed constables from Oxford, though, as back-up,' she added, 'So there will be five of you on the ground, with DI Graham coordinating.'

'And will you be joining us yourself, ma'am?'

She didn't answer that.

'I am disappointed that you are all so resistant to the idea. This is our best chance to catch the Butcher's Row gang. I had expected more enthusiasm.'

'We just like to know what we are getting into, ma'am, that's all,' DS Pardoe said soothingly.

Owen wondered if the others were as doubtful about this as he was. Josh was still new enough to be excited by the whole thing, and probably the uniforms from Oxford would be the same. Graham wasn't saying much, but Collins couldn't tell whether that was because Rowena had commandeered his case or because he objected to the whole idea. And of course Sally was opposed to the DCI's ideas as a matter of principle.

When Rowena had left, the others returned to discussing the gang and their victims.

'They've got a definite MO. Have you noticed that none of the victims was seriously injured? I mean, a broken finger, a couple of cracked ribs, concussion, but nothing life-threatening,' Josh said.

'They mean to frighten, rather than hurt, you think? Or it could be just coincidence.'

'The choice of victims isn't arbitrary, though. All male, all the same age group.'

At twenty-five, Dutton was the youngest, while Khan at thirty-four was the oldest.

'The similarity in age is surely simply a result of when and where,' Pardoe said.

'No, actually, if you picked men randomly at closing time, you'd expect them to be younger, wouldn't you? Lots of students out and about at that time, but they pick out the grown men. In fact, it looks as if they are deliberately attacking the kind of people who are least likely to be attacked in the circumstances. No women, no minors, no one with a disability,' Sally said.

'Are you suggesting the Butcher's Row gang have a kind of target audience?'

'It looks like they do. And if that is the case we have our strategy for Thursday,' Graham concluded.

Owen found that suddenly everyone in the room was looking at him.

'What?'

'If we are to do this undercover thing...' Sally said.

'Yes?'

She grinned at him. 'Then you are the perfect bait.'

After the meeting Collins went to see Matt Fielding, to tell him, as gently as possible, that he could be Victor Farndale's grandson. Fielding took it as calmly and sensibly as could be expected. In fact, perhaps a little too calmly.

'You'd already spoken to him, hadn't you?' he asked Sally when he saw her on Thursday morning, 'That's where you went the other day.'

'He's got a right to know. I thought it would be better coming from me.'

'You're probably right about that. And he didn't let on that he already knew. You okay with discussing the case?'

'Sure. In fact, I've got some questions. What I don't understand is that when Matt was left at St Bride's they couldn't trace his parents. Someone must have known about Maite and her baby. She had him in hospital. There's a birth certificate for Mateo de Burgos, born 17 December 1986, naming her as the mother and Robert Farndale as the father.'

'Yes, but that was all official, she never tried to hide her condition, and no one would have expected her to abandon her child. You have to remember she wasn't trying to keep Matt's existence a secret. She did everything new mothers are supposed to do, went for prenatal check-ups and all that, and she told her doctor the baby would be looked after by his grandparents after she was gone, so there was no reason for concern on that score. If she hadn't been so conscientious, perhaps the doctor or the nurses would have linked the foundling to the single mother they had attended to, but for all they knew that baby was safe with Victor and Annabel.'

'Yes, that would explain it, I suppose. So, next question: has this got anything to do with Victor's murder, or is it just a side-show? Because whatever Rowena thinks, I haven't forgotten what we're supposed to be investigating.'

'I don't know. Surely if the murderer wanted to punish anyone, they would have killed Robert?'

'Unless they made the same mistake as I did, and assumed that Victor was the father.'

He knew there was really only one possible suspect if this was the motive, and he knew Sally realised it too. Matt.

'But he's got an alibi,' she said.

'Yes. There are other possibilities, though. Victor was the only one apart from Robert who knew about Matt. Maybe someone wanted to keep it that way.

'Why would anyone want to keep Matt's parentage a secret? To protect Robert?'

'Or to protect their own inheritance. Does Matt's share reduce anyone else's bequest enough to matter?'

'No, he would get a lump sum, just like the other grandchildren. That means about eight thou less for each of the children, but compared to what they're getting that's peanuts.'

'Yes, but imagine if Victor had lived into his nineties and all his children had kids of their own. They would have felt the difference then.'

'You're saying that perhaps someone just thought it was time for him to go?'

It did sound unconvincing, put like that. 'All right, all right, I'm just speculating. Anyway, let's first get Rowena's obsession with the Butcher's Row gang out of the way. It's unlikely that Victor's murderer will strike again, after all. I'm taking the afternoon off, since I'll be working tonight. You might as well do the same.'

Of course he didn't really take the afternoon off. While he waited for the new bookcases to arrive, he tried to work out on paper which suspects they had left in the Farndale case, assuming that Robert was telling the truth and it wasn't him. First he made a list of possible motives.

- revenge for Annabel's death
- financial gain from bequests in will
- retribution for what happened to Matt
- suppressing truth about Matt
- personal animosity

In the first case, the twins were the obvious candidates, and it would explain their eagerness to shift the blame onto others. And he wouldn't put it past them to be working together. But the fact remained that they had been either out of the house or accompanied by their respective boyfriends when the deed was done. Still, he put them on his list. Ursula Westmacott was another possibility if revenge for Annabel was the motive, but unlike the twins, she said she had never believed Victor responsible for his wife's death. Had Adam Rokeby's visit changed that, and had she decided to swap Victor's pills on the spur of the moment? It was a possibility, so he put her name down as well.

The second motive was more straightforward, and had the largest number of possible suspects. Everyone except Eliza would be substantially better off than before Victor died, but only Robert and Bettina and Juliette appeared to be in urgent need. Mr Taylor was coming to read the will at Ulvercott next week, and perhaps that would throw more light on the situation.

The motives relating to Matt were there only for the sake of being complete, he didn't really believe the cases were related.

The last motive was the vaguest, but it seemed to fit the killer's MO. What had Sally said? *What kind of murderer chooses a method with only a middling chance of success?* The answer was one who was more intent on causing harm than producing a practical result like instant riches. The trouble was that it also meant that it wasn't obvious what the killer gained by it, and as long as all the Farndales maintained that they had got along with Victor, there was no way of identifying them.

At this point the doorbell rang, and his help was needed to carry the new bookcases up the stairs.

33

Around midnight, Collins found Sally on the corner of Butcher's Row and Crown Street, looking fed up.

'How're you doing?'

'Never mind paid overtime, I could have earned a fortune tonight. Sparsely dressed lady hanging around under a lamppost is never alone. Stay around for a bit, will you? I've had enough drunken propositions to last me a lifetime.'

'I've only had two,' Collins said ruefully, making her laugh.

'Do you think this is actually doing any good?' she wondered.

'We'll know at closing time.'

Each of them was supposed to walk 'home' on their own, all in different directions, in the hope that either the gang would consider them an easy target, or they were in time to spot them closing in on someone else. But they couldn't cover every lane and alleyway, and there was a real danger that some innocent victim would suffer instead. Not to mention the chance that the gang were all at home watching telly, he thought, shivering in his light jacket. He set off down Butcher's Row again, and he heard Sally's heels clicking away behind him.

Sally looked at her phone so she wouldn't have to notice all the minor breakages of the law going on around her. The others showed up as coloured dots on the town plan on her screen. Josh was strolling down Minster Street, the constables from Oxford where in the Newmarket, Owen was on the corner of Butcher's Row and Walker Alley, and she was in front of the Hollow Crown pub. DI Graham was coordinating from a car discreetly parked in Crown Mews. They took it in turns to separate from the crowd and go off down the darker alleys, in the hope that the gang would notice and follow. The whole thing felt a bit ramshackle to Sally. Sure, this wasn't a big city, and any one of them could reach any of the others within minutes, but the problem was that it took much less than that to kick someone in the head. There were also other problems. She had already had to break up a fight and call in uniform to arrest a pickpocket, and Josh had run into a couple of mates who wouldn't understand that he couldn't join them for a pint. Their brief had been to be unobtrusive and see if anyone was behaving suspiciously. As far as Sally could see, *everyone* was.

And it was bloody cold, too. She was just contemplating dashing over to Costa to get a coffee when her phone beeped the 'all officers' signal. She looked at the map on the screen. There was a pulsing green dot on Tanner Street.

Sally ran.

Owen had pushed the pre-set button as soon as he saw the two hooded figures stepping out from the nameless cul-de sac off Tanner Street. There were footsteps behind him, and he knew there would be two others cutting him off from the other end of the street. He looked anyway. They were closer than he'd thought, also in dark clothes and hooded. On of them, the tallest, stood in front of him, invading his personal space, daring him to react. He raised an arm, put it on Owen's chest, a gentle push.

Owen balled his fists at his side, making an effort to control the instincts drummed into him by endless self-defence classes. He could have grabbed the arm to bring down his assailant, but his three friends would have been in there kicking but not screaming before he could have said 'you're under arrest'. Self-defence was no use four against one. Why was it still four against one? What was keeping the others? He kept his eyes resolutely on the figure in front of him, who still hadn't spoken.

'I wouldn't do this, you know,' he said, surprised at how steady his own voice sounded.

It wasn't the leader, but the one to his right who spoke. 'Look, not this one mate. He's fuzz. Let's just scarper.'

Did that voice sound familiar? No matter, the others would be here soon. 'You're not going anywhere, you're under arrest, all of you.'

'I don't think so.' The leader's voice was quiet and confident. 'I think I'll enjoy beating up a copper. Are you scared, little policeman?'

I'm not that little, Collins thought absurdly. He shook his head. Why was everything happening so slowly? He shouldn't have time to think about his opponent's choice of words.

'Not even a bit scared?' the taunting voice repeated.

And suddenly he *was* scared, and everything happened very quickly. A harder push this time, and he almost lost his balance. An arm swung at him from behind, a painful impact to his shoulder. He lashed out himself, instinct taking over now.

'Really,' the familiar voice hissed again, 'Not this one. He'll have back up, let's just go.'

He started to back away, followed by his silent friends, while Collins grappled with the leader. As he came in for another blow, Collins twisted behind him, got his arm around his neck and twisted upwards. Hands grabbed at his arm to pull loose the stranglehold. But his opponent was strong, and managed to pull Owen off his feet and throw him. He aimed a final kick at Collins's ribs before he hared off into the darkness.

'Halt!' came an impressive bellow from the end of the street. Was that Josh? As he scrambled to his feet, Collins could see the two constables from Oxford sprint past after his assailants.

'Blasted heels!'

Sally came hopping towards him on only one shoe. 'Are you all right, sir?' She reached out a hand to help him up.

'I'm fine. Shame I couldn't hold him here. I think he went to police self-defence classes.'

'Never mind that, I just hope the others will catch them. Too easy to get lost in the crowd.'

Sally tiptoed to where her other shoe had fallen and reluctantly pulled it on again. 'Could have been here a lot quicker if Rowena hadn't insisted on party clothes,' she muttered.

'They just would have run earlier,' he said, 'They're playing a game of hide and seek with us. They were never going seriously hurt me knowing there were other officers arriving any moment.'

It was true, he realised. The gang had never inflicted life-threatening injuries and they weren't going to start with a police officer. But that argument had not been available to Collins while he was surrounded, and for a moment there he had really thought that there was little chance of getting out alive. Which probably explained why he felt a bit unsteady right now.

Sally had noticed that too. 'You're shaking,' she observed, 'Better pull yourself together or Josh'll never take you seriously again.'

He managed a smile. 'Not sure he ever did. Can you call Graham and tell him to stand the others down? It doesn't matter if they don't catch the gang tonight, because I know who they are.'

Sally raised her eyebrows at this, but she did as he asked, before rounding up Josh and the others and marching them all into the Newmarket Bar, where she demanded they be served hot, sweet tea, which was probably the strangest thing to happen there for a long time.

'So talk to us,' she said, after they had found what passed for a quiet corner in the town's most popular night spot.

'It was just like the others described. They came from different directions, surrounded me, all in silence. But one of them recognised me, and he told the leader they should leave me alone. *He* was clearly all for beating me up regardless, but I recognised the voice of the one who knew me.'

'If you're trying to rack up the suspense, it's working,' Sally said.

'I'm not, honestly,' he said, sipping his sweet tea. It did help, to his surprise. 'It was Mortimer Farndale.'

34

It was nearly three o'clock when Collins got home to Flanders Alley. He took a shower, made another cup of tea, and sat on the settee for a bit, thinking about what had happened. There was a book lying on the side table, and to take his mind off things he picked it up. It was called *Bloodlines: Murder and Succession in the Visigothic Kingdom* by Stuart Tanner. The existence of the Visigothic Kingdom had escaped him until now, but there was a helpful map and a timeline. He looked at the introduction and found that it was surprisingly easy to read. Apparently getting your hands on a crown was once a reasonable motive for murder.

He was woken by someone saying his name in a concerned voice.

'Owen?'

He straightened up, and found he had a crick in his neck. 'Ow.'

'Why are you asleep on the sofa? We have this place upstairs, called a bedroom. It's got a bed in it.'

'I know. I just sat down for a minute. What time is it? Oh.'

He'd been asleep for over an hour. Dominic took the book from his unresisting hands. 'One could be forgiven for thinking that you get enough murder by day.'

'I thought it was quite interesting, actually.'

'I'm reviewing it for *The Historian*, but I'm sure Stuart will be glad to know it has a broader appeal. Seriously though, why are you asleep here on your own? What time did you come in?'

'Threeish.'

'You could have woken me up.'

'No need for both of us to lose sleep.'

Dominic grabbed him by the shoulders. 'Owen, what happened tonight?'

As succinctly as he could, he described his encounter with the Butcher's Row gang.

'Were you in danger?'

'Probably not as much as it felt like.'

'You were the bait in the trap.' There was something cold in Dominic's voice which he hadn't heard there before.

'We all were.'

'I thought you were there to run to the rescue of the victim, not be the victim yourself.'

'To be honest, so did I. I never thought it would work like Rowena imagined.'

'Is that part of her job description, sending her DIs to be beaten up on the off chance?'

'I don't think there really was much danger. And we got a result. Why are you so upset about this?'

'Owen, if you ever come in cold and shaking because you ran to the rescue when your job required it, I'll be very proud of you. But if you come in cold and shaking because your boss doesn't know how to do *her* job…'

So that was the ice in Dominic's voice. Anger. He hadn't seen his lover angry before. He wasn't sure that he could handle it at this point.

'It wasn't so bad, truly. And you should have seen Sally and Josh. They were brilliant.'

'I'm sure they were. You must tell me all about it in the morning. All you are allowed to, I mean. I'm assuming you are off to the station again first thing?'

'Yes. I'll need to give a statement. That makes a change.'

Dominic pulled him to his feet, and they went upstairs to bed, but not yet to sleep.

DI Collins wrote four names on the whiteboard in the CID room.

- Mortimer Farndale
- Gareth Swift
- Natasha Mitchell
- Scott Mitchell

'That's our gang. You were right all along, Sally.'
'About what? Not that I don't like hearing you say that, mind.'
'Mortimer and his friends weren't playing FIFA that Friday night. Or not all night.'

For a moment she couldn't think what that had to do with anything. Then the penny dropped. 'The night Samir Khan was attacked! So when we came asking for an alibi for Victor's murder...'

'They used an alibi they had already agreed on beforehand.'

'And you're sure Tash Mitchell joined in the attacks?'

None of the victims had mentioned a female attacker. Maybe they hadn't noticed. Or maybe they didn't like to admit they had been beaten by a girl.

'I'm sure one of the people surrounding me last night was a woman. Different silhouette when she ran away.'

Sally had thought Owen seemed pretty shaken after being confronted with the gang, but apparently not so shaken that he couldn't notice something all the other victims had missed.

'Well,' DI Graham said, 'If you're sure, let's bring them in. Want to do the honours?'

'It's your case,' Collins equivocated.

Sally looked from one to the other. 'Oh stop being gentlemanly, you two. Collie and I can pick up Mortimer, while DI Graham and Josh collar the others.'

It was only when they were getting into the car that she realised that she had called her superior officer by his nickname in front of the others. A good thing that Rowena hadn't been there to hear it.

At first, when they brought in Mortimer Farndale, he tried to deny everything.

'I expected you to be more eager to confess,' Collins said, after letting him protest for a bit.

'Why on earth would I want to do that?'

'To put it simply: admitting that you were beating up Samir Khan on January 31 gets you out of a murder charge.'

'What?'

'You provided a false alibi when I asked you where you were on the night your father's medication was tampered with. That looks suspicious to me.'

After that, Mortimer became positively eager to talk, and it was plain sailing.

'The first time I was drunk. I thought we all were. I realised later that Swift hadn't been drinking at all. But me and Scott were properly soaked, you know, at the stage when you think anything at all is funny. So when they started pulling that guy around it was like a silly game, watching him stagger about. He was just as drunk as we were. Only it wasn't a game. I kept seeing his face, afterwards. He didn't understand what was happening, and we just went on kicking him.'

'What happened then, Mortimer?'

'Swift said 'that's enough'. I don't think Scott and Tash would have listened to anyone else, but they stopped just like that. Then Swift told Scott to call 999 and we left him there.'

'And then a week later you did it again. And again.'

'Yeah. The fourth time was when Tyler joined us.'

So he *had* been running away from the scene that night. 'Tyler Whitaker? How did he come to join you?'

'He was with the gardeners who come to ours every Thursday. One time I was in the kitchen when Jacqueline asked them in for tea. I got to talking to Tyler, turned out he loves FIFA but had no one to play with, so I asked him to join us sometime. He's much better at it than Scott or Tash. Anyway, when he had played with us a few times Swift said he could join us when we went out.'

'Isn't Tyler Whitaker a bit wrong side of the tracks for Mortimer and the Mitchells?' Sally asked, 'I mean, they've all got A levels, office jobs, rich parents... You know, *privilege.*'

He could see what she meant. Tyler was also a lot younger than the others, and the only one who wasn't white.

'I'm sure Scott and Tash thought so, but it was Mortimer who befriended Tyler, and his father was a foundling, came from nowhere. That's one thing you can say for the Farndales, they're not snobbish. And I bet Swift just loved to get his claws into a new victim. You heard how Mortimer spoke about him. He would do everything Swift told him to.'

'Yes, he's clearly the leader. Have we got hold of him yet?'

'No, he's gone to ground. He's not at work – Colin Mitchell is proper pissed off – and there's no one home in Court Street. Court Street! I should have thought of that when I first interviewed him. That's how the gang managed to disappear so quickly after the attacks, of course. They didn't mingle with the crowd, they just went to Swift's flat. But it is only a matter of time before we find him. Let's hear what Tyler has to say first.'

'I liked playing FIFA with Mortimer and his mates,' Tyler said, 'That's how it all started. When Swift suggested the other thing, I just sort of went along.'

'How did you meet Mortimer Farndale?'

'I work for a horticultural firm. It's horrible. The other week I had to scoop dead fish out of a pond! *And* it was freezing. Anyway, we do Ulvercott House on Thursdays, and the lady would give me a cup of tea in the kitchen. One day Mortimer was there, and we got talking.'

He was a bit of a chameleon, Tyler Whitaker. A background check had thrown up two cousins who had done time for dealing and theft, and his mother's brother, Chase Tabares, had once been quite notorious in a small-town way. Collins remembered him from his time as a uniformed PC. Tyler's street slang, unlike Mortimer's, sounded genuine. But he was well-behaved enough to be allowed in Jacqueline Whyatt's kitchen, and he had never been in trouble before, not even for shoplifting.

'You've kept your head down until now, Tyler. We've nothing on you, and you must have been exposed to temptation before. So why, when Swift proposed this little venture, did you suddenly give in?'

Tyler shook his head. 'The guys at work, they're always on at me. When Swift explained what they were doing, I though maybe we could do Art or Dougie. I really wanted to hurt Dougie. And Swift said, why not, if we come across one of them. But we didn't, we found this bloke I didn't know at all, and the others really went for him. And so did I. But it wasn't, it wasn't...' he broke off.

'Yes?'

'It wasn't like they'd said at all.' Tyler took a deep breath. 'It didn't feel good or anything. And so I ran away. Swift called me the next day, just before you lot came, to remind me to keep my mouth shut. He said they could easily do to me what they'd done to the bloke we attacked. So I didn't say anything. And it were only the once!'

'I think once was quite enough for Ben Dutton.'

'Is that his name? Is he badly hurt?'

Mortimer Farndale hadn't asked that.

'Not so bad, considering. You have given him a bad scare, though. That is also a kind of damage.'

'Yeah, that was what Swift wanted.'

'Damage?'

'No, to scare them. He *is* scary, you know, Swift. The others did everything he said. I should have got out when I noticed that.'

'But you didn't.'

'I just liked hanging out with them. It was chill. It was somewhere to go.'

'But after the assault on Ben Dutton you decided to get out. That was sensible of you. Why didn't you tell us the truth when we picked you up, though?'

'I don't want to go to prison, do I? And I wasn't going to do it again.'

'If you had told us the truth last week, we could have prevented the others doing it again as well.'

It was obvious that Tyler had never considered this. He'd just wanted to get as far away from all of it as possible. Odd boy.

'What is going to happen now? Will I go to prison?'

'What will happen is that Swift, Mortimer Farndale and the Mitchells will be tried for various charges of assault and actual bodily harm. Since you were a minor at the time the offence was committed, you will be dealt with by the youth court.'

It would probably mean community service for Tyler – compared to the premeditated attacks perpetrated by the four adults, his half-hearted participation in one of them was small fry. But it wouldn't hurt Tyler to believe that prison was a realistic prospect for someone who assaulted random strangers.

'I am *so* glad I'm not eighteen anymore,' Sally said, after they had let Tyler go with a referral to the Youth Offending Team.

'I'm fairly sure there's a nice boy somewhere under all the confusion.'

She gave him a look that reminded him of Bridget. 'What was it this time, the big brown eyes?'

'Hey, just because I'm biased doesn't mean I'm wrong. Or did you think that was a calculating criminal mastermind running rings around us?'

'Nah, you're probably right. Mind you, after spending time with the Farndales, most other people start to look nice.'

35

'Where is DS Holmes?' Rowena asked, when she found Collins alone in the CID room.

'Sitting in on DI Graham's interview with the Mitchells,' he replied.

'Shouldn't Robbins be doing that?'

'Josh was at school with the Mitchells, Peter doesn't think he's ready for that yet.'

'Seriously? DS Holmes knows a suspect socially, and so does Robbins? What is wrong with you lot?'

Collins shrugged. 'It's not a big city. I actually met my own partner on a case.'

'You're joking, right? I thought he was university lecturer.'

'He is. Long story.'

Rowena was looking at him as if she still couldn't quite believe it. But then she often looked like that, affronted that the world wasn't behaving exactly as she expected. What on earth had possessed her to join the police? You had to be able to tolerate a certain level of unpredictability in this job.

She shook her head. 'This place... Well, if you see Sergeant Holmes, tell her that I want to see her in my office ASAP.'

'Yes, ma'am.'

That sounded ominous. He had expected the DCI to be pleased that her plan had worked, they had four-fifths of the Butcher's Row gang in custody, after all, but she hadn't even said 'well done'.

Sometimes he really missed DCI Flynn.

Sally was in an interview room with DI Graham and Scott Mitchell and his solicitor, having exactly the same conversation they had just had with Scott's sister Natasha, and feeling frustrated. They all knew Mitchell and his sister had been part of Swift's gang, but as long as they kept denying it, they would be forced to let them go. She just couldn't find a crack.

'So you've all known each other for years. What did you think of Mortimer bringing in Tyler?'

A shrug. 'They were both addicted to playing FIFA. Sure, I play myself, but I'm not obsessed, like. Not like those two. It was a bit pathetic.'

'He's a good-looking boy, Tyler. Maybe there was another reason Mortimer wanted him to join your little gang,' she probed.

'Not likely. Mortimer has been trying to get off with Tash since she was fifteen. Like I say, pathetic.'

Sally didn't think the one excluded the other, but she let it go. In the end it didn't matter how the gang had got together, only what they had done. And both Scott and Tash were still maintaining that they had never assaulted anyone in their lives. She was sick and tired of hearing 'no comment'. Did they really believe they could get away with it, with Tyler and Mortimer willing to talk? Their smug solicitor appeared to think so.

Things didn't get any better once she got out of the interview room. Josh came up to her to say that DCI Dixon wanted to see her right away. He looked worried.

'Sally, I have been thinking about what happened last Tuesday. On reflection, I think it is better if you step away from the case. I should have realised sooner that you are too closely involved. Have a few days off, take a breather from it all.'

'You could have told me this two days ago,' was all Sally could think of to say.

'As I said, on reflection...'

'Bollocks. You couldn't have pulled off the op without me. That's why you waited.'

Rowena's lips pressed into a thin line at this. 'You heard me. You needn't come in on Monday. Don't make things worse for yourself.'

Five minutes later, Sally walked out of the doors of the Petergate nick, not sure what had just happened. Was she supposed to see this as an unexpected holiday? Or was this the beginning of the end of her career in CID? She didn't know how much clout DCI Dixon really had. If her superiors took her as seriously as her subordinates did – which was not at all – there might be nothing to worry about. But if Rowena reported last week's incident through the official channels, they might have to act... It was no use speculating, but she couldn't help it. Considering possible scenarios was second nature, after all, looking at things from all angles, asking questions. And then not being sure of the answers. There was one thing she was sure of, though. If she was no longer on the case, there was nothing to stop her going to see Matt. It would take her no more than a hour to get to Southampton, if the traffic was good.

'And?' she asked, as soon as she saw him.

Matt just nodded.

'Robert is your father?'

'Yes, it's a match. I got the test result this morning.'

'Fancy that. You've got family.'

'Quite. Although I'm not sure that having Robert Farndale for a father is a reason to rejoice. But there is so much that makes sense now, everything they told me at St Bride's. When and how I was found, what I had with me. I was in a carrycot! I had new clothes, a clean nappy, I even had a cuddly toy. It was always so clear that someone had cared for me, and then I was left. It was such a huge question, and now I understand.'

'Your mother gave you a cuddly toy?'

'Yes. Wait, I still have it.'

He went into the bedroom and came back a moment later with a little stuffed fox, its plush a little thin now, its cheeky muzzle shiny with age.

'This is Zorro.'

'And you had him as a baby? You had that stuffed toy all the time, and I never saw it?'

'I took him everywhere when I was little. But I wasn't going to let on I still had a soft toy to the younger kids, was I now?'

Suddenly Sally felt herself tearing up.

'I'm sorry, it's just— Maite, she did everything she could for you. She would have been such a good mother, Matt. She *was* a good mother. And you are so much like her. So sensible and kind. You're nothing like Robert.'

Matt fingered Zorro's worn ears, and gave her a sad smile. 'Do you think—' he broke off, untypically hesitant.

'What do I think?'

'I'd so much like to have children of my own. Do you think I'd make a good father?'

She smiled now. 'I don't think it, I know it. And you'd better be, because I haven't had the best example of parenthood myself.'

They sat there with the little fox between them, laughing and crying at the same time.

'Will you be using the name she gave you?' Sally asked at length.

'Well, I suppose Mateo would still get shortened to Matt over here, so that's not a problem. But I've been called Fielding all my life. Wouldn't it be confusing for people I know if I suddenly became De Burgos?'

'Bugger them. What do *you* want?'

'I'll have to think about it, but as long as it isn't Farndale I'm all right. Look, do you mind if I talk shop? Your shop, I mean? It's just that I thought of something.'

She'd nearly forgotten her own predicament. 'Erm... I'm not actually on the job at the moment.'

She explained about Rowena's sudden decision to suspend her after all. 'But never mind that, I can always call Collie if I've got new intel. What did you want to tell me?'

'I've been thinking about the Farndales. Not who could have done it, but who might know something. Do you remember Kayleigh Mercer?'

Sally hadn't thought about Kayleigh for years. She had been at St Bride's for a few months before a foster family was found for her.

'She fancied herself a spy, didn't she? Always trying to hear what was being said in the staff meetings.'

'Exactly. Robert and Bettina's daughter Bella is like that. Observant, always knows things no one has told her. And she likes secrets. If she saw anything, she won't come forward out of a sense of duty. You'll have to tempt it out of her.'

'I saw her at her school, but I didn't get much response at all. You think she knows more than she's saying?'

'Undoubtedly. Whether it is anything useful I couldn't say.'

'Right. You ever hear what became of Kayleigh Mercer?'

'She's an investigative journalist now.'

'That makes sense. And I'll pass what you said about Bella on to the DI. I don't think he expects me to sit quietly at home, whatever Rowena decides.'

36

Owen spent Saturday afternoon at the Farndale Museum, listening to Dominic giving an account of life in the middle ages, illustrated by objects from the museum's collection. The audience was mostly elderly, and apart from Noah, who was helping Dominic, he was the youngest person present. He spotted Ursula Westmacott sitting in one of the front rows, but he made sure she did not see him. He could do without Farndales for a few days. But when the lecture had finished, he bumped into Adam Rokeby.

'Inspector Collins, good to see you. Are you interested in local history?'

'Well... I'm interested in historians. That one, specifically,' he said, nodding in Dominic's direction.

'Oh?'

'He's my partner.'

Rokeby smiled. 'I see. So you're not here in an official capacity?'

'No. Unless there's anything you need to tell me?'

'Oh, no. I just wondered, since you haven't made an arrest, I take it my fears about my cousins proved groundless?'

'Yes, I'm glad to say you have now been officially classed as a red herring.'

'Good. Thinking ill of people doesn't come easily to me. Shall we get a glass of wine?'

'Sure, and I'll introduce you to Dominic.'

Thinking ill of people did appear to come easily to the Farndales. Or rather, they did not appear to be bothered by the idea of harbouring criminals in their midst. Last week both Robert and Mortimer had been arrested, but when Collins saw them all together at Victor's memorial, the family appeared to have closed ranks. Robert sat straight and solemn between his wife and Nora, every inch the chief mourner, and Mortimer was flanked by the twins, who whispered to each other across him. Of course, this wasn't the best place to observe their reactions. Possibly angry words had been spoken at Ulvercott House. Collins couldn't imagine Ursula, for one, letting Robert's behaviour pass without comment. But for now, during the ceremony and the gathering at the Radetzki afterwards, the Farndales presented a united front.

He watched them all as they circulated, greeting old acquaintances and distant family members, remembering Victor, and wondered, not which of them was acting – with the possible exception of Nora, they all were – but which of them had chosen the most difficult part. Was Oliver deliberately ignoring his father? Why was Ursula talking so earnestly to Katarzyna Krupinska? Was Eliza just too good to be true?

Electra and Antigone were talking animatedly to Colin Mitchell, waving wineglasses about. Were they celebrating their father's life, or his demise?

'Owen!'

Collins turned to see Jake beckoning to him from behind the buffet table, in respectable waiter's black this time.

'Jake, good to see you. I'm sorry I've had no time to chat.'

Jake shook his head. 'This is work. Your work I mean. Those girls over there, the sisters, are they Victor Farndale's family?'

'Yes, his twin daughters, why?'

'I saw them before. They had lunch here last month, those two and two other young women. I remember because they were talking about poisoning someone, and they didn't exactly lower their voices.'

Owen looked back at Electra and Antigone. He didn't think they knew how to lower their voices.

'Why didn't you say before?'

Jake shrugged. 'I didn't know who they were then. I never met Simon's girlfriend, remember? And it sounded so fantastical, I thought maybe they were organising a murder game or something. You know, when you all have to find out that it was 'the stepdaughter, with poison, in the study'. A couple of us from Odd Jobs have been asked to act in one of those next month. Should be fun.'

'But this was in earnest. Can you remember exactly what they said?'

'I was in and out of here all the time, so I caught only snatches, but I'm sure one of them said 'you'd have to find pills that look exactly the same' and another 'you could do it at anytime, and be nowhere near when it happened'. That was the skinny one, I thought I saw her here as well, but she's gone now.'

Juliette. Owen wondered who the fourth member of their little lunch party had been, but Jake couldn't help with that.

'She was sitting with her back to me, I didn't see her face. She had shoulder length blonde hair, but that doesn't really help, does it?'

There were plenty women of that description here. Bettina, or Poppy perhaps? But it could just as well have been a friend of the twins, unrelated to the Farndales.

'Can I have some more wine here, please?' One of the guests was waving an empty glass at Jake.

'You have work to do as well,' Collins said, 'Thanks Jake, you've been really helpful.'

'No problem,' Jake said, hurrying over with a bottle, 'Laters!'

Back at the station, Collins tried to figure out what this new information meant in practical terms. He should never have taken Antigone's word for it, he realised. This explained why Sunita hadn't recalled Victor proposing the murder method himself. The girls had discussed it among themselves afterwards, and creatively elaborated the memory. And he had heard and read every subsequent account of the Christmas dinner in the light of what Electra and Antigone had said, more fool him. It was only they and their cousin who had taken a step further, and one of them had reminded the rest of the family the day after Victor died, giving the impression that everyone's thoughts had turned to murder when the patriarch threw out a careless remark about his medication.

Could it be a conspiracy between the three of them? But that meant that Juliette's hostility to the twins had to be an act. No, it was more likely that they had simply talked, and only one of them had decided to test the theory.

Antigone, Electra or Juliette? Or their blonde mystery guest?

He wished Sally was there to share this with. He told Josh, who stopped typing a witness statement long enough to look suitably impressed, but it just wasn't the same.

37

Matt

from: matt.fielding@usouthampton.co.uk
to: sallyholmes2@mailspace.com
re: The Will!

Hey Sal,

That's the first time that I've been present at the reading of a will, and if it is always like that I think I'll give the next one a miss. I've described it as accurately as I can remember, but this being the Farndale family there was a lot of cross-talk and interrupting each other. Not sure it throws new light on your case, but there is one big surprise in there. Here goes.

Present in the dining room of Ulvercott House: Eliza Farndale, Ursula Westmacott, Robert and Bettina Farndale, Oliver Farndale and Poppy Alexander, Nora Farndale and Sunita Mahajan, Electra Farndale, Antigone Farndale, Mortimer Farndale, Algernon Taylor (solicitor) and myself (thirteen people in total, a fact which Antigone remarked on). This is what the solicitor said:

'Twenty-thousand pounds outright each to the Farndale Museum and to St Bride's Children's Home. There is a small monetary bequest to Mrs Jaqueline Whyatt, whom I shall inform personally. The remainder of the estate after death duties is shared among the family, as follows: each of Mr

Farndale's grandchildren – that is, Mr Oliver Farndale, Miss Bella Farndale, and Mr Matt Fielding – will receive the sum of fifty-thousand pounds, to be held in trust until the age of twenty-one in the case of minority. The same provision has been made for Mr Farndale's niece by marriage, Miss Juliette Westmacott. Mr Farndale's sister-in-law, Miss Ursula Westmacott, is also to receive fifty-thousand pounds outright, in recognition of all she has done for the family. Mr Farndale's capital and other liquid assets, less the aforementioned bequests, are to be equally divided between his children, to whit, Robert, Elinor, Electra, Antigone, Mortimer and David Farndale.'

Here Mr Taylor paused to let it all sink in, and Electra jumped in with a question.

'But what about the house? Do we all get a share of that, or does it go to Eliza?'

'That is the last item of the will. The house and its contents are left unconditionally to Mr Oliver Farndale.'

And then all hell broke loose.

Electra and Antigone turned to Oliver and demanded to know what he thought he was playing at.

Oliver himself did not say much, apart from stating several times that he had not known Victor intended to leave him the house. Poppy went all 'stand by your man' and kept telling the twins to leave him alone, which appeared to embarrass him. When they'd finally stopped calling Oliver names, they turned to interrogating Eliza about what Victor could have meant by this.

(After a murder, two arrests, and the juicy fact of my existence, I thought that nothing else could possibly shock the Farndales. I was wrong.)

Surprisingly, it was Bettina who brought her outraged in-laws back down to earth by pointing out that they had all just been told that they would be receiving substantial sums of money, and that it was disgraceful to complain of not getting more.

Robert said that it was not the money, it was the principle of the thing, and Victor had been very unfair in singling out Oliver, which is a bit rich from a man who chose to abandon his own child rather than take responsibility. I wonder if all his talk about Victor being a bad father is a form of transferral or projection or something? He still completely ignores my existence, by the way. But you can tell the others are less likely to listen to him now they know what he's done. And so they ignored his accusations of unfairness and simply returned to interrogating poor Oliver until Ursula put a stop to it.

Never a dull moment at the Farndales...

Matt

PS As if the past few weeks have not been unreal enough, Victor's will means that I'm to have an unexpected fifty-thousand pounds in the near future. It hasn't quite sunk in yet.

38

The email was forwarded with a note from Sally saying 'read this and call me'.

'I thought you talked to Mr Taylor about the will? Why didn't he mention that the house would go to Oliver?' Collins asked, when he did so.

'I've been thinking about that. I spoke to Martin, the younger Mr Taylor, right after Matt turned up at the station, and I think what he gave me were the contents of an earlier will. Algernon, the elder Mr Taylor, who visited Victor at home, is semi-retired, he wouldn't have been in the office first thing to tell his son about the change, if there had been amendments recently.'

'Hmph. I suppose in the end it doesn't make much difference to the question of motive. They all inherit their share, and none of them is so much in need of money that they would need the house as well.'

'It could be the murderer acted out of anger at what they perceived as unfair treatment.'

'Surely that is a motive for killing Oliver, not his grandfather,' he argued, 'And for keeping Victor alive as long as possible in the hope that he would change his mind again.'

'This gives Oliver a motive, though, doesn't it?'

'But according to Matt he didn't know about the bequest. It's a pity we weren't at the will reading, I would have liked to see his reaction.'

'But even if he knew about it, why be in such a hurry?'

'Perhaps he thought the solicitor's latest visit meant that Victor intended to change his will *again*. Poppy and Oliver saw Victor on their own, didn't they? What if he told them then?'

'But that was on Saturday. And however ambitious they are, surely they wouldn't have been stupid enough to kill him directly after they heard what they stood to gain.'

He looked over Matt's account again.

'Juliette wasn't there?'

'Yeah, I noticed that too, so I called her to ask why not. Yes, yes, I know, I'm out of line. But I did, and she says that she'd had quite enough of the twins looking all smug and that she'd wait for the solicitor to contact her.'

'That young woman certainly has a chip on her shoulder. Anyway, thanks Sally, for the info. I hope you'll be back here in person soon.'

'So do I.'

'I had no idea, honestly,' Oliver said, when Collins went to talk to him at Ulvercott House, 'But now I understand why grandfather wanted to talk to me when we were here over Christmas...' He shook his head. 'But then, it wasn't such a strange subject for us to talk about. How to use your assets and things like that. You see, my father isn't a very good businessman. He just started out with a lot of money and made a lot more in a time when it was practically impossible to fail. Now he's overstretched, lumbered with properties he can't shift. So I got to thinking what I would do in that situation. It's no use trying to sell things there is no market for. But that doesn't mean that the properties are useless. I told dad he should let the city flats on Airbnb, that way you're at least making money instead of paying a firm to keep squatters out. But that's something he just doesn't understand. Well, that's his loss. And it is the country houses that have the real potential, anyway. There are always people looking for event locations. I should know, Poppy talks of little else. So I talked to grandfather about what I'd do with the houses dad can't get off his hands, and he asked me what I would do with Ulvercott if it were mine. I didn't think he was serious!'

'And what did you answer?'

'I said I would offer the old offices in the west wing as conference rooms, and hire the main house out as a wedding venue. It would need some refurbishment, of course, but that investment would earn itself back soon enough.'

Until now Collins hadn't seen why Eden Kingston had looked so happy talking to Oliver Farndale. But now, with the boy all fired up with enthusiasm for his project, he suddenly did. His father's dominant personality – not to mention Poppy's – made it look as if Oliver had no ideas of his own, but that was clearly far from true. Clever Eden to have spotted that. Or it could just be the public school good looks, of course.

'And you would go into business with Poppy?'

For the first time Oliver's enthusiasm for the project seemed to flag. 'It would make sense, wouldn't it, since she is going into the wedding business?'

It was his plan, and he wanted to keep it to himself, not have Poppy run it, that was clear. But Oliver was soon off on another tangent. 'You would need a good manager on the spot, of course. I wonder if Jacqueline would like to stay on?'

Collins left the young man to his plans and went to talk to his fiancée.

'It's a piece of good fortune, and very generous of Oliver's grandfather. That's all there is to it,' Poppy said, rather defiantly, when asked about the will.

'Good fortune?' he echoed.

'I mean we'll be able to realise our plans earlier than foreseen,' she said airily.

He noticed that Poppy assumed that she would share in Oliver's good fortune. And of course if they were to be married, that would be the case. But it wouldn't surprise him if for Oliver his 'piece of good fortune' would prove an excuse to rethink his position. Being ostracised by his family could have that effect on a young man. That was none of his business, though. He was satisfied that Poppy had not known about the bequest beforehand, and that was all he wanted to know. In fact, it seemed that apart from the solicitor, Victor had told only one person of his plans.

'I knew,' Eliza said, a little shame-faced, 'But he was so insistent I wasn't to talk about it. Once he knew that it was only the pills keeping him alive, he started thinking about who was to follow in his footsteps. He had a private talk with each of his children and grandchildren in the past few months, even David and Bella. He wanted to know if any of them had plans, the kind of plans he had himself when he was young, if any of them had some endeavour he wanted to boost from beyond the grave.'

'But he did not tell them that was what he planned?'

'He wanted honest answers, not sales pitches. Victor loved his children, but he had no illusions about them. If he chose to leave the house to Oliver, it must be because Oliver had the soundest plan for using it.'

'But Victor must have known it would cause some resentment.'

She shook her head. 'That was his blind spot, I'm afraid. Victor never confused money and affection, and couldn't see that others did. He thought they would all receive too much to complain, and in material terms of course that is true. It would have been a business decision to him, but his children will see it as favouritism. Unexpected favouritism, at that, because he hadn't shown any preference for Oliver before. If he had been playing favourites Nora would have scooped the jackpot.'

'Did he talk to you about his reasons?'

'No, but I know he kept notes. Would those be useful to you?'

She emailed them that afternoon, and he read them through at once. Victor had given a brief description of his conversation with all his children and grandchildren. The last entry dated from just before his death. Collins wished Sally were here to discuss them with. He had the feeling that brief as they were, there was something important in there, but he just couldn't put his finger on it.

39

Victor

Robert
I asked Robert first. He is always so insistent on his rights as the eldest son. I'm afraid that until now he has assumed that he will come into the house, and he was upset when I asked what he'd do if he would get it. But he rallied enough to answer that he would modernise it in the hope of finding a rich buyer.
He doesn't know I know, but his company doesn't have the means to take on such a large project, even if he uses the rest of his inheritance to pay off his debts. He needs to scale down, and find a way to make his existing assets pay. But Robert's way with a problem is always to hope that going on as before will make it go away. He is not getting the house.

Nora
When I asked Nora the same question as Robert, she simply refused to entertain it.
'We don't want the house, dad. Sunita and I are perfectly happy as we are. To be honest we're not sure what we'll do with the money, when it comes to it, apart from pay off the mortgage. And we'd prefer it if you hung on for a bit longer.'
That's my girl.

Electra & Antigone
The twins, when asked – separately – what they would do with the house, answered – identically – 'Live in it, of course!'

No sense of proportion, just like their mother. There are eight people living here now, Jacqueline included, and even with the west wing closed off there's plenty of unused space. I want this place put to good use, and not just as a backdrop for my daughters' sense of theatre.

Mortimer
'I don't know.'
That's what Mortimer said when I asked what he would do with the house. I wonder if he really doesn't know, or just isn't saying? He likes to hoard his secrets, my second son. I can never get much out of him. I wonder if it would have been different if his mother had lived. I should have been a better father to him then. I fear it is too late now.

David
Also 'I don't know', but more understandably in his case. He's only fourteen. I won't burden him with this place. I know Eliza wants him to be a normal teenager, not just the millionaire's kid. I wonder what he'll be like when he grows older. He is so different from either Robert or Mortimer – all my children are more like their mothers than like me. Not a bad thing, perhaps, but I would like to pass this place on to someone who at least thinks a little like me.

Oliver
Finally, a bit of enthusiasm, and a bit of sense. I don't believe Oliver had ever thought about Ulvercott before, but when he set his mind to it, he came up with a viable plan in minutes – wedding venue, conference space. He's clearly been learning from his father's mistakes. In my investing days I'd have given him a loan on the strength of it. As it is, he's the best candidate for the house so far.

Bella

I spoke to my granddaughter today, which is hard going for both of us. It's a pity she's such a silly girl. She's got brains, but no application. I had hoped that that school would knock some sense into her, but there's no evidence of that so far. Perhaps I'm being harsh – she's only fifteen. When I asked what she'd do if she had the house she said: 'What would I want with a stupid old place like this?'
What indeed?

Juliette

You can imagine the outcry if I should leave Ulvercott to someone who isn't even a Farndale, but I thought I had best talk to Juliette anyway. She reminds me so much of Olivia, although there is something calculating about her that Olivia lacked. Or perhaps I have forgotten that my wife had her calculating side. It is so long ago now. She said, as I knew she would, that she would use any money she came into to finance her research.

Matt

I can't be sure yet, of course, but I had the chat with Fielding as well, even though I had already made up my mind that it would be Oliver. I haven't changed it, although I enjoyed my talk with Matt.
'I've never thought about it. Sell it, I suppose, and then take my time to think about what to do with the money.'
Very down to earth, Matt Fielding, which is just what Electra needs, of course. A pity that it won't go through if my suspicions prove correct.

40

Collins wanted to talk to DCI Dixon about Sally. He arrived early on Tuesday especially for that purpose. She hadn't consulted him or Peter, just gone off and sent Sally home, leaving only four of them working two cases. A heads up would have been nice. Or a chance to speak up for his colleague. But when he walked into her office on Tuesday, he found it empty.

'DCI not in yet?' he asked Pardoe in the CID room.

'Haven't seen her, sir. You've heard about Sally?'

'Yes, that's why I wanted the DCI. I may not have the same idea of what constitutes a small team as Rowena, but I am now SIO in a team of one. She could have bothered to tell me, at the very least. And I could have put in a word for DS Holmes.' He found that he wasn't even trying to give Rowena the benefit of the doubt anymore.

At that point DI Graham arrived, and addressed the room in general.

'Look people, before we move on to the case reviews, I have something to tell you. The Chief Superintendent has suspended DCI Dixon pending an inquiry into the handling of last week's operation. I've been appointed acting DCI for the duration. Questions?'

'Is it only DCI Dixon, or are we all to be investigated?' Pardoe asked.

'Headquarters are asking questions about the wisdom of setting up the operation in the first place, and about whether all reasonable safeguards were in place. These were decisions that were the DCI's responsibility. There have been no concerns raised about the conduct of individual officers during the operation.'

'That's good.'

No one looked forward to having the internal inquiry team visit, not even if they were not under investigation themselves, but it could have been worse.

'I have spoken to the Chief Super only briefly,' Graham continued, 'But it may not even come to a full-scale inquiry, if Rowena agrees to step down herself. We'll see. Now, let's get on with the order of the day. I'm afraid I'm expected at headquarters today and tomorrow, but I'm sure you all have plenty of actions to be getting on with.'

As the others got on with their work, Graham took Collins aside.

'Look, I wanted to say I'm not happy with the way they have overlooked you. You are the obvious candidate for acting DCI, you were here long before me.'

'But you have the experience. If you are okay with returning to your old rank, then they made the right call.'

He meant it. He had no desire to deal with the aftermath of the Rowena Dixon shambles. Or to repeat her mistakes.

'I don't know that I ever want to be DCI,' he added, 'I'd rather go on doing something that I'm good at than try being something I'm not cut out for. And I'm not at all sure that Rowena's job is what I'm cut out for.'

'In my old nick, with your abilities, you would have been DCI already,' Graham said with conviction.

Owen scoffed. 'You don't know the half of it. I've made some questionable calls in my time. Decisions for which I could have been suspended. I don't know that I would have done any better in Rowena's place.'

'Then why weren't you suspended?'

'I got a result. Several, in fact.'

And I had Bridget Flynn on side, he thought. But that he would keep to himself.

'Well, there's the difference, for a start.'

'We did catch the gang as a result of the op.'

'Owen, the only reason we caught them eventually is that you recognised Mortimer Farndale's voice. It was pure chance, and she can't dress it up as anything else. The operation was ill-judged and badly executed, and that was her responsibility.'

'Did you speak to her beforehand?'

'Of course. I advised her strongly against it. She had plenty of chances to make the right call. Don't feel too sorry for her.'

'I won't,' Collins assured him, 'Still, I'm not in a hurry to become a DCI. I'm not sure I fit into the hierarchy very well. Rowena was on at me about doing most of the interviews myself, and all I can say is that I like doing it. I like it where I am now.'

'There's nothing wrong with that. Have you talked this over with your partner?'

'Only in a very general way. He knows I'm not aiming for Chief Constable, at least.'

'You haven't been together very long, have you? If there's anything I've learned, when there's something big going down on the job, talk it over with the home front. Doesn't matter if that's your wife, your boyfriend, your kids; they're going to have to live with it as much as you.'

'I suppose that's true. What does your wife think of you going back to DCI so soon?'

'She worries. But she also knows I'm unhappy away from the job. And on that subject, as my first act as DCI, I have asked Sally to come back.'

'That's great. But are you authorised to do that?'

'She wasn't actually suspended, Rowena just asked her to stay home for a few days. And it's easier to do without a DCI than a DS, if you have a murder case to solve.'

'And that's you telling me to got on with it,' Collins concluded.

He found Sally in the CID room, reading up on the developments of the last couple of days.

'I see you didn't suddenly rush ahead in my absence,' she said drily.

He was just about to explain his spectacular lack of headway when the desk sergeant called up to the CID room. 'I've got a Mr Swift here who says he wants to confess. Is DI Graham – I mean the DCI, of course – still here?'

'No, he just left. Put Mr Swift in an interview room, please. DC Robbins and I will be along shortly.'

Gareth Swift was seated at the table, lawyerless at his own request, enjoying, and that was the right word, a cup of canteen coffee. He looked entirely relaxed.

'So, Gareth.'

'Swift,' their suspect said, 'No one calls me Gareth.'

'Swift, then. Why did you turn yourself in?' Collins asked, after he and Robbins had identified themselves for the recording.

'Didn't want to draw it out. You'd find me eventually, better you find me on my own terms.'

'No, no,' Collins said, 'You misunderstand me. *Why* did you turn yourself in? What crime do you imagine you are to be charged with?'

But Swift wasn't so easily put off balance.

'Imagine? Well, I imagine grievous bodily harm. Or is that not what you call it these days?'

'It will do. Would you care to tell me to whom, and when?'

'In the past four weeks, my friends and I attacked and injured Sylvester Murray, Samir Khan, Conor Briggs and Ben Dutton respectively, and in the early hours of Friday the 20th we attempted to do the same to you, Owen Collins. The last was a mistake, of course. We had no intention of harming an officer of the law. Please accept my apologies.'

Collins was pretty sure it hadn't been a mistake. There was no way Swift hadn't recognised him. But that didn't matter right now.

'And why did you do this? Do you enjoy hurting people?'

'I enjoy being on the winning side.'

'Bit of a rigged contest, four against one. Or five, as the case may be.'

Swift shrugged. 'It's not about numbers. It's about fear.' He smiled, unpleasantly. 'Have you arrested the others? Are they afraid now?'

'We have spoken to your associates. Our concern now is with who did what. Whose idea was it, Mr Swift? Scott Mitchell's? Mr Farndale's?'

'Mortimer? He couldn't think his way into a girl's knickers,' Swift scoffed, 'Whose idea do you think it was?'

'For the tape, Mr Swift.'

'Mine, all right, the idea was all mine. The first time it happened by accident. We were just jostling this guy around a bit, but when he got scared I saw the others were ready for some action. So I hit him.'

'Without provocation.'

'Because he was there,' Swift drawled. 'He'll live, won't he? We just gave him a beating.'

'And then what did you do?'

'Told Scott to call an ambulance and the others to get the hell out of there.'

Mortimer had mentioned that. 'You called 999 yourselves?'

'Yes. Bit of risk-control there. You can go to gaol for things like that.'

Collins decided to ignore that. 'Continue.'

'I could see the others were all fired up, they were likely to start blabbing if they saw any of their mates, so we went to my place and spent the rest of the night boozing. Then if they wanted to forget, they could forget. But they didn't. When I messaged them if they wanted to see some more action, they jumped. All of them.'

The story was the same for the next two victims, with the only difference being the temporary addition of Tyler to the gang.

'Right,' Collins rose, 'Interview terminated at 11:45. Constable Robbins will escort you to your cell.'

'Hold on. Don't you want to know why we did it?'

'You have admitted to doing it. That's enough for us.'

But he sat down again anyway. This man had wanted to beat him up in public. He did want to know why. And Swift was obviously going to tell them whether they wanted to hear it or not.

'People are dumb. They just live their lives, never stopping to think it could be all over in a moment. There are terrorists out there, there are floods and storms, planes crash, trains derail, people die. But that means nothing if you live in a boring little town like this. People feel safe here. But that's just an illusion. Nowhere is safe. The ground state of being for humans is fear. Fear of the darkness, inside and out. But we've forgotten. People think they can keep the danger away, they think they are in control of their nice provincial lives. They are complacent: stupid, ugly and complacent. I wanted to bring the fear back. The random terror of the jungle, regardless of colour or creed. One moment you're here, gone the next. That's what life is really like. I could see it in their eyes, when they were down, they knew the truth, then.'

How much brooding had gone into this, how much resentful watching before some trigger turned it into violence?

'And you don't feel the fear when you're fighting?'

'I'm not afraid,' Swift protested, 'I know what's out there. I know the darkness. It can't be worse than what I can imagine.'

'I hope not.' Collins didn't know what else to say. What did you do with a confession like this?

'But *you* were afraid, weren't you? I could tell you were afraid,' Swift gloated.

It was true. When he'd been confronted with them in that dark empty street, he had been afraid, with an old, elemental fear. It would be useless to deny it. He could see Swift thought it meant he had won.

'Oh, yes I was afraid,' he said, 'Do you think it's something to be proud of, not being afraid? Fear is human, Gareth.'

'Fear makes you weak. And don't call me Gareth.'

'No. Fear makes you brave. And it's fear that's got you nicked. Not yours, mine. And I'm proud of it.'

41

As soon as Owen got home he told Dominic about Rowena's suspension.

'At this rate you'll have no colleagues left by the end of the week. Are you relieved?'

'Of course I am. The situation was becoming impossible. It was time for headquarters to jump in. And it does mean we get Sally back.'

He got himself a beer from the fridge. 'To be honest, I think they were planning for this all along. Give Dixon enough rope to hang herself with, and then pull her out at the first hint of trouble and tell her in the nicest possible way that maybe she isn't ready yet to be a DCI. I did wonder why they assigned Graham to us in the first place.'

'You mean they put her here specifically to fail? That's...'

'Unethical, would you say?'

'I suppose that is what I would say, yes.'

He shrugged. 'It can be very hard to put the finger on why someone is unsuitable for a job. This way, there can be no question. And she did get a chance to get it right.'

Dominic didn't look convinced. 'I can imagine that when it's putting someone in a lecture hall full of students and see if they sink or swim. I would have thought that doing so with a police department is plain irresponsible.'

'They probably counted on the CID ticking over for the time being whoever was in charge. I mean, Pardoe will deal with things in exactly the same way whoever is in the office, and Robbins still consults the manual when he thinks we're not looking. HQ took a calculated risk that we'd survive a few weeks of Rowena, and we did.'

'And I thought academia was a cut-throat world.'

'Never mind the job now. You wanted a hand unpacking your books?' He opened the nearest box. 'How do I know what to put where?'

'Fiction in the living room, non-fiction in the study,' Dominic said, 'I did *try* to pack them separately.'

'And after that?'

'Fiction alphabetically by author, non-fiction by subject. I'll do that myself. Why, were you hoping I'd organise them by colour?'

Owen had never had so many books that he needed to think about how to organise them. 'That might look nice in the living room.'

'Let's get them all unpacked first.'

By the end of the afternoon they had all the books out of the boxes and on the shelves, and Owen found that he hadn't thought about murder or assault for hours.

'Right,' Dominic said, looking around the study. 'Good job well done. I think we deserve a reward. Let's go out for dinner.'

'As long as it's not the Radetzki.'

They were enjoying their starters at the Cathedral Hotel when DS Holmes called.

'Sally, what is it?' Owen asked, making an apologetic face at Dominic.

'Bella Farndale's had an accident with her bicycle, she's in hospital.'

'Is it serious?'

'Bruised ribs and a broken collarbone. She'll live.'

'And you're calling me because…?'

'Someone tampered with the brakes.'

'Right, do you need me there?'

'No, I've got everything in hand. Matt called me after it happened. He and Oliver went to pick up the bike and noticed the brakes. They haven't told anyone else yet.'

'Good. So what now?'

'I'll have forensics collect the bike, and we can talk to the other Farndales tomorrow, hear what they've got to say for themselves.'

'What was Bella doing at Ulvercott anyway? Shouldn't she be in school?'

'They gave her time off to attend the memorial, she was supposed to go back to Overdene tomorrow.'

'Is she well enough to be interviewed yet?'

'No, she's out for the count. I'll ask the doctor when we can see her.'

'Fine. Thanks for keeping me in the loop.'

He knew Sally would have things well in hand, but the attack on Bella bothered him. He hadn't expected anything like that at all.

While Collins was enjoying his night out, Sally was in the infirmary, talking to a harassed-looking doctor. She wondered how long the woman had been on shift.

'I must say, it makes a difference from seeing you lot after the Butcher's Row gang have been at it. Why are you here anyway? It was a simple accident. We're confident that she'll be well enough to go home when she wakes.'

'Don't you need to keep her under observation for the night?'

'Funny, that's exactly what her aunt said.'

'Nora Farndale?'

'No, an older lady called West-something-or-other.'

'Westmacott.' So Ursula was also concerned about Bella's safety.

'Anyway, no,' the doctor said. 'She didn't get knocked on the head or anything. She's just sleeping off the anaesthetic from when we stabilised her collarbone.'

'Let me rephrase that,' Sally said, 'It would be really helpful if you could keep her under observation for another night. Because if you keep her here I'll know she is safe while I try to find out who did it.'

It was probably only because the doctor was too tired to argue that she got her way.

The next morning, she and Collins interviewed Bella at Ulvercott, with Ursula present as her appropriate adult.

'I understand you have already given a statement to a constable after the accident, but I'd like to ask you a few more questions,' Sally began, 'You see, there was something wrong with the brakes on your bike, and we're trying to find out whether someone sabotaged them.'

'Really? You mean someone was trying to kill me?' Bella sat up eagerly, and then lay back again with a flinch. 'Ow.'

'Bella!' Ursula interposed, 'This is not one of your detective stories. It's not something to be pleased about.'

'Yes, of course, Aunt Ursula. So what do you want to know?'

'Who knew that you were going for a ride yesterday?'

'I think I said something on Monday, after the memorial.'

Right. With the maximum number of people present, like the Farndales always did.

'And the bike, where do you keep it?'

'In the old stable. It's locked, but the key is on a hook in the kitchen, anyone can go in there. Mortimer's and David's bikes are also in there.'

'And everyone knew which bicycle was yours?'

'I suppose so. Mortimer's bike is much too high for me, and anyway, it isn't a mountain bike. And David hardly ever uses his, it wouldn't surprise me if the tires were flat.'

There was nothing else Bella could tell them to throw light on her accident, and they left her alone with her aunt.

'I think that woman has done more than anyone to keep that family together. They all snipe about each other, but never about her. Aunt Ursula is above all blame,' Collins observed.

'Suspiciously so?' Sally asked, feeling that he was scraping the bottom of the barrel there.

'Oh no, I didn't mean that. Although one can imagine her executing a perfect murder if she thought it was the right thing to do. We'd never catch her – much too efficient.'

'She'd also be good at shielding someone else. I've been thinking. The only one here who is actually related to Ursula by blood is—'

Sally fell silent as they came out into the hall, seeing that they weren't alone. The rector, Adam Rokeby, was just getting out of his coat.

Collins greeted him like an old friend. 'And what brings you to Ulvercott today?'

The rector looked troubled. 'Ms Westmacott asked me to come, she wanted to talk. I am afraid I cannot tell you what about.'

'Adam, if it has a bearing on the case...'

Rokeby shook his head emphatically. 'Nothing, I promise you. Not everything is about murder, remember?'

Sally thought Collie accepted that much too easily. Hadn't they just been talking about Ursula's behaviour? But the DI's next question put that out of her mind again.

'How is Matt getting on with his new family?'

She waited until they were back in the incident room before replying. 'It helps that he already knew them, I think, but it is still awkward. His existence forces them to acknowledge that a Farndale has hurt another member of the family. Although Antigone's line is to blame Matt for bringing it all to light. That woman lives in another world.'

'And Bettina?'

'I think perhaps this was just the nudge she needed to acknowledge that her marriage is on the rocks. And at least she talks to Matt, she's been all right. Robert simply ignores him. Oliver is curious, they spent a lot of time talking together yesterday. But I think the rest are suffering from family-scandal overload, they're still coming to terms with Mortimer getting arrested, and now the attack on Bella.'

'And what about Electra?'

'She alternates between finding it all hilarious and being down in the dumps because she and Matt are not together anymore. Um...'

She concentrated on her laptop screen, not looking at him.

'Something you need to tell me, Sally?'

'Like what?' she asked, knowing it was useless.

'Like who has taken advantage of the fact that Matt is officially single again?'

'Yeah, all right, we think maybe we can make a go of it. All on the quiet right now, though.'

She was still looking at her laptop screen, but she knew anyway. 'And you can stop looking so smug!'

Collins dutifully tried to assume a neutral expression while Sally brought a picture of Juliette Westmacott up on screen, next to one of Victor's first wife.

'To get back to business, here's a scenario,' she said, 'Juliette returns from France, no one at Ulvercott has seen her for years. Victor sees a young woman who is the spit of his first wife – he mentions that in his notes, remember – and makes some inappropriate move, or perhaps just says something unwise about her looking so much like Olivia. Juliette is horrified that the man she thinks of as a kindly grandfather is seeing her in that light, and can't bear to be near him. But she still wants her inheritance. So she dutifully keeps turning up at family occasions, stressing her dislike of the twins to hide her real emotions, and waits for an opportunity to speed Victor on his way. When the twins come up with their foolproof murder method during lunch at the Radetzki, she has found it.'

Collins didn't think it rang quite true where Victor was concerned, but he had to admit that as far as they knew Juliette it was possible.

'We've got no proof at all, though. What did Bella know? And did Juliette have the opportunity to tamper with the bike? She wasn't here when the will was read,' Sally said, picking holes in her own hypothesis.

'No, but she was at the memorial. Easy enough to nip back here. I'll ask Ursula or Jacqueline if they've seen anyone.'

'Fine. All right if I knock off here?'

'In a hurry to be somewhere else?'

She made a 'more or less' gesture with her hand. 'I'm seeing Matt, as a matter of fact.'

Collins couldn't be sure, but he thought he was probably looking smug again. He liked having the old Sally back.

42

After Sally had gone home, Collins had a quick word with Ursula.

'You haven't told me much about your niece. She is your younger brother's child, is that right?'

'Juliette? Yes, she tends to remain in the background, especially compared to Electra and Antigone. When they were younger, I think there was some resentment on Juliette's part. Like she is now, her parents were archaeologists, and lived a rather hand-to-mouth existence, travelling from dig to dig. Ulvercott was the height of luxury by comparison, and the twins made her feel it. But she loved Victor. He was the reason she kept coming back here, I think. He encouraged her career, and it was partly because of her enthusiasm that he took on the refurbishing of the museum.'

Ursula set down her coffee cup. 'Perhaps I don't know her as well as I should, though. She is my family, after all, not Victor's, like everyone else here – there is a strong resemblance to my sister at that age. But she spent a lot of her time in France from when she was eighteen, and she is a rather reserved person. There must be much I do not know about her.'

'She called herself the poor relation,' he recalled.

She shot him a quick glance. 'It is a large step from resentment to murder, Inspector.'

'But not a giant leap. Did you see her on the Friday afternoon before Victor died?'

'I caught her having a cigarette on the terrace. That must have been at around half past five, just after she arrived. If you are asking if she had the opportunity to slip upstairs unseen, well, I'm sure I can't say.'

They were at Ulvercott again the next morning, talking to a convalescent Bella. The patient was being looked after by Ursula, Bettina and Jacqueline, and was clearly enjoying the attention. With Bettina's permission they were talking to her daughter alone, having argued that after the attack the girl might not actually feel safer with a familiar adult present. In reality, they were simply hoping that she would speak more freely without her mother or aunt looking on.

'So Bella, I bet you see a lot of what goes on at Ulvercott, even though you don't live there. Is there anything you can tell us about your cousin Juliette?'

He waited while she contemplated whether to throw the dog a bone. They were in luck.

'She was stealing. I saw her when we were all here for grandfather's birthday. And again at Christmas.'

'Are you sure?' Sally asked.

'Of course I am sure,' she said scornfully, 'Mortimer never carries a wallet, he just stuffs bills in his jacket pocket. I saw Juliette go through them in the cloakroom. And the twins are just as careless. Another time I caught her rooting around in Tig's handbag. Said she was looking for a packet of tissues because she hadn't any of her own.' She sniffed, obviously unimpressed by the lie. But did she understand what Juliette had really been looking for?

'And no one else knew about this? Didn't people complain about money going missing?'

'I don't think it was much, not so much that someone like my aunts or uncle would notice. I think she probably just enjoyed hurting them a little. And of course she is always short of money.'

'And did she know that you were on to her?' Sally asked.

'She must have known I suspected. Do you think she is the one who tampered with my brakes?'

Bella appeared to find this more thrilling than threatening.

'Do you?' Sally asked Collins, as soon as they had returned to the incident room.

'It's a feeble motive. All she had to do if Bella accused her was deny it, her word against that of a girl who delights in stirring up trouble. Can Bella really have scared Juliette so much that she wanted her out of the way?'

'It's possible that Bella is not telling us everything.'

'It's more than possible, it's probable. In fact, she may have brought up the theft just to divert us away from what it is she really knows. What I don't understand is why, if she knows who killed Victor, she can't just tell us.'

'Because she wants to solve the murder herself, of course. Stealing a march on the detectives.'

'That could be it,' Collins said. 'And Bella was watching, she said she saw Juliette go through Antigone's handbag. That may be quite true. But what if she wasn't after money at all? What if it was a pack of contraceptive pills she wanted?'

'And if Bella saw her take them...'

'Then she would know Bella was onto her.'

'Why would Juliette not use her own, though?'

'She uses a brand that's orange in colour.'

Sally rolled her eyes. 'Trust you to know a thing like that.'

'I asked every woman in the house whether they were on the pill as soon as Dr Nakamura told me about the amount of oestrogen in Victor's system. Antigone is, but she admitted to being rather slapdash about taking them.'

Sally looked at the timeline again. 'According to her statement Juliette arrived on the five o'clock bus on Friday, but Bella said she saw her earlier. And we know the timing of Bella's visit is accurate because the school clocked her back in.'

'So Miss Westmacott may have lied about her time of arrival.'

'Or Bella is making things up. I wouldn't put it past her.'

'We'll need to check the CCTV on the bus. I'll put Robbins on it.'

Two hours later he was back in the incident room, where Jacqueline had put Juliette as requested. He turned to close the door behind him and saw that he had been followed. 'Hello Foundling,' he said, bending down to stroke the cat's back.

'My, aren't you good at making friends,' Juliette said sourly. 'I do wish Jacqueline would keep that beast out of this part of the house. Cats make me sneeze.'

After a brief internal struggle duty won, and Collins put the cat, not the woman, out in the corridor.

'You had some more questions?'

'About your arrival at Ulvercott on the thirtieth. According to your statement, you arrived on the five o'clock bus.'

'That's right.'

'But according to Bella Farndale she saw you when she came to pick up her stuff, and she was long gone by five o'clock.'

'Haven't you noticed by now that that girl is a terrible fantasist?'

Whether that was true or not, he knew the cameras on the bus didn't lie. Josh had been quick.

'We have other ways of checking,' he said, 'Were you here before five o'clock on Friday, Miss Westmacott?'

She shrugged. 'I may have been. Perhaps it was the four o'clock bus. I didn't look at the time. Is it important?'

Collins couldn't decide whether that was a naïve or a supremely self-confident question. But she didn't expect an answer.

'I mean, I could have as easily slipped upstairs after five as before, couldn't I? And unlike some, I don't spend all my time here hobnobbing in the downstairs sitting room.'

She was right, of course. Juliette certainly had the opportunity, but beyond some very circumstantial suspicious behaviour, they had nothing on her. Some careful probing into her relationship with Victor didn't elicit anything except platitudes.

He reported his lack of result to DS Holmes.

'You think she's too unconcerned to be guilty?'

'Not necessarily. I'd say overconfidence suits the profile.'

'Like Swift, believing he can stay in charge even under arrest.'

'Yes. But if Juliette is like that she is better at hiding it. I wish Bella would tell us what she knows. It must be truly incriminating for the murderer to risk attacking her. Perhaps when she is back at school she will feel safe enough to tell us the truth.'

'I'll call Ms Saunders,' Sally said, 'I can go there on Friday.'

When Collins went into the kitchen to ask Jacqueline if she had noticed anything suspicious on Sunday, he found Eden there, with Oliver Farndale. The latter got up at once and made a gracious exit.

Eden snorted, unimpressed. 'I think I'll bring him into class some time: 'The effects of privilege on the male brain'.'

'You like him, though.'

'That obvious, am I?'

'And so is he. I don't think he usually spends much time in the kitchen.'

'You may be right. But he was only asking me what they are paying me for helping Jacqueline. I think he's writing a business plan, and doing some field work. He almost didn't believe me when I told him.'

'Is it so little? I thought Odd Jobs paid well.'

'They do, for unskilled work. It's certainly better than what I got when I was behind the counter in Boots. But I'm afraid Oliver has grown up thinking in another order of magnitude. His old man thinks he's being cheated when he gets less than a million for a property. My parents are still paying off the mortgage they took out before I was born.'

'The problem is that when people with that kind of money go down, they go down hard.'

'Is that a subtle way of saying that I've been chatting up a murder suspect? Because obviously this wasn't hopeless enough already.'

'No, I was thinking of Oliver's father.'

'Yes, I heard about that. Mr Fielding is his son, isn't he? What a mess. I keep telling myself Oliver must take after his mother.'

She was silent for a bit, and then asked, 'Isn't that difficult? I mean, you must have opinions – feelings – about all these people, and you have to always consider that the worst explanation is the right one. I can just say, no, no way, not him, but *you* can't.'

'Yes, that is difficult. And people don't always forgive us for thinking the worst of them after they have been proved innocent.'

'Must be hard for your sergeant.'

He didn't say anything. Honestly, the girl was worse than Jake!

'Sorry, was that supposed to be a secret?'

'Eden, do me a favour, keep your observations to yourself, all right? There's someone here who doesn't scruple to silence anyone who knows too much, and I don't know who it is yet. Until I do, just try not to upset them.'

43

Before they could pursue the Juliette angle further there were other matters to attend to. While Peter Graham was acting DCI, most of his work ended up with their one remaining inspector, and Collins found himself dealing with the fallout of the assault case at the same time as trying to manage his own investigation. The county were running a new restorative justice programme, in which victims of robberies and violent crimes were given the opportunity to meet the guilty party, and the Butcher's Row gang were deemed eligible. The notion met with a varied response from victims and offenders alike. Scott and Tash Mitchell, and the smug solicitor hired by daddy, were still maintaining they were innocent, and it took only one look at his interview transcripts for the probation officer in charge of the programme to decide that Swift was not a suitable candidate for reconciliation meetings. Things were different with Mortimer Farndale and Tyler Whitaker. Femi Akande, the probation officer, thought that since they had both admitted their guilt, they would respond to being confronted with the consequences of their actions. Collins could see her point. But the victims also needed to agree. Sylvester Murray wasn't interested and just said 'No, thank you'. Samir Khan, on the other hand, nearly jumped out of his skin, saying he had no intention of extending the hand of friendship to the racist scum who had come after him, and no amount of talking could convince him that Swift and his gang had chosen their victims randomly.

'What else do you call it, when four white guys beat up an Asian man?' he demanded angrily.

At which point even Ms Akande – female, IC3 – gave up. 'One of those guys was a woman,' she said, 'And not all of them were white. You have made your position clear, Mr Khan, we wish you all the best with the healing process.'

Conor Briggs was another matter. He jumped at the chance to meet Mortimer Farndale, and spent fifteen minutes bellowing at him that he had been a stupid little shit to throw away the advantages in life he, Conor, would have given his right arm for. Whether it had given Briggs closure Collins couldn't say, but it certainly appeared to have had a salutary effect on Mortimer, who looked very thoughtful the next time Collins saw him at Ulvercott.

And then there were Tyler Whitaker and Ben Dutton.

Things were a bit different for Tyler, because he had been present at only one of the attacks, and he had still – just – been a minor at the time. Ms Akande suggested a more informal approach, and so on Thursday afternoon Collins and Holmes took Ben Dutton to Rivergate Park to meet one of his attackers. There really was no need for the sergeant to be there as well, but they were both curious about what would happen. They were quite a party, because Tyler Whitaker was accompanied by his aunt, whom they had encountered on the Abbey Hill case last year.

Once introductions had been made the young men looked at each other, clearly not knowing what to say next. Then Tyler nodded his head at Ben's face and asked, 'Did we do that?'

Dutton touched the bruise below his left eye. 'No, that's a new one. Aikido practice. In theory I am supposed to be able to defend myself. It is only when there are five of you that I get into trouble.'

'I'm sorry.'

'Are you?'

Tyler nodded again, fervently.

'Why don't you tell me?'

They moved off to sit on a park bench, while Mrs Whitaker and the detectives hung back.

'I hadn't expected to see you here, Mrs Whitaker,' Collins said.

'It's Gail, remember?' she said, 'And Tyler wouldn't be here at all if it weren't for me. I'm afraid my nephew's parents distrust the police, and anything to do with it. Someone from the Youth Offending Team came to talk to them, and they wouldn't even let him in. But I know Tyler wants to make amends for what he's done, so I offered to come along if he didn't want to go alone. His parents don't know he is here.'

She sighed. 'It's ironic, really. My husband's brother and his wife are quite strict. Tyler is their only child and they are always checking up on where he's going, who he's meeting, as if he's still twelve years old instead of almost grown up. But they approved of Mortimer Farndale, they thought he was a responsible, respectable kind of person.'

'And you didn't?'

'Oh, I knew nothing about any of this until Tyler was arrested, I don't see much of them. But, well, I don't know if it's because of having two girls myself, but I would definitely have wondered what a man nearly ten years older from a completely different social background wanted with my kid, you know what I mean?'

'I certainly do,' Collins agreed, 'But that part was actually quite innocent. Mortimer and Tyler got together over a shared love of playing FIFA. But Mortimer was already tangled in Swift's web, and he dragged Tyler in with him.'

Gail's nephew and Ben Dutton were talking quite animatedly now. They were too far away to hear, but the body language wasn't hostile, quite the opposite, in fact. After a few minutes they got up and came back to where the others were standing.

'Is it all right if I take Tyler out for a meal, to talk it over properly?' Ben asked Collins. He turned to Gail, 'I promise I'm not angry with him, I just want to understand.'

'Is that what you want, pet?' she asked her nephew, 'You don't have to.'

Collins thought that if Tyler had ever had any street cred, the last of it slipped away when his aunt called him 'pet' in front of the police.

Tyler shot a quick glance at Ben and then nodded.

'All right. But do come home at a reasonable hour, won't you? Let's not worry your mum any more than necessary.'

'I'll make sure, Mrs Whitaker,' Ben said, 'Thank you. Inspector, is there some legal reason we shouldn't do this?'

'Just remember there's still a court case to come.'

Tyler flinched at that, and Collins could have sworn he saw Dutton suppress the impulse to put an arm around his shoulders.

'What have we done?' he asked Sally, as they watched Ben and Tyler walk away towards the Rivergate Pizza Express.

'Well, I suppose it makes a change from 'police officer falls for witness',' she said, raising an eyebrow at him. Sally's mood had improved a lot since Rowena had been removed from the office.

44

Sally was driving south on the M3 on her way to Overdene House, to talk to Bella Farndale again. If only the girl could be convinced to share her secrets...

She enjoyed driving, it gave her time to think. About yesterday's conversation with Electra and Antigone, for example. Being fairly sure by now that the sisters were not implicated in the crime, she had asked why they had tried to incriminate Matt or Simon. Did they know who was the real culprit?

'Oh, we have no idea,' Electra had replied, 'But we know it must have been one of the family, and we wouldn't want any of us to go to gaol, would we Tig? Not even old Nora.'

Was that what Matt had seen in Electra, Sally wondered, that rock-solid, unwavering family loyalty?

That was something she just didn't get. She saw it all the time, of course, she knew it existed, but she could not understand it. How could a mother, in the face of the evidence, keep insisting that her son was 'a good boy, really'? Why would a father look away or make excuses when his daughter was obviously a thief? How did people convince themselves that there was an innocent explanation when a loved one came home with a garbled story and blood-stained clothes? Did loving someone mean always thinking the best of them? Wasn't it more kindly in the end – not to mention law-abiding – to acknowledge a loved one's faults instead of denying them? And was the blood-tie really so important? The twins' familial protectiveness clearly didn't extend to Juliette, who was Robert and Nora's cousin, not theirs. It was all a bit depressing.

Just as she turned her car into the drive of Overdene House, DI Collins called.

'Are you at the school yet?'

'Nearly. Why, has something turned up?'

'I've had an idea. I need you to do something for me.'

Sally listened while she parked the car, and agreed to the change of plan. Tara Saunders was waiting for her in the school's entrance hall.

'Good afternoon, Sergeant. I understand you would like to talk to Bella again?'

'Ms Saunders. To be honest, I'm not quite sure. I need to check something for my boss first. This is going to sound a bit strange, but does this place have an attic?'

'Well, yes, of course. Do you need to have a look?'

'If you would be so kind.'

The attic was large and cold, and obviously not in use for anything official. Sally saw some furniture under dust sheets, and what looked like a double bass without strings.

'Are the girls allowed up here?' she asked.

'No, but of course some of them do come anyway. We try to allow them their secrets. It's not good for children that age to be too much supervised.'

Sally nodded. 'Well, I need to look for something.'

'I'll leave you alone up here, in that case.'

'No, don't go,' Sally said, as she pulled on a pair of latex gloves, 'It won't take long, and I'd rather have a witness.'

'All right,' Ms Saunders said, sounding bemused.

As well she might, Sally thought, as she started walking the length of the attic, looking up at the beams. She'd been right, it didn't take long. At the fifth window along, she noticed a wobbly little stool that was less dusty than the rest of the furniture. She carried it over to the nearest beam and stood on it, feeling across the top until her hand encountered something papery. She held up her phone and photographed the thing in situ before taking it down.

'What have you got there?' Ms Saunders asked.

'Bella Farndale's diary,' Sally said, looking inside the cover to check. 'Ms Saunders, I came to talk to Bella, but I will need to check in with my DI before proceeding. There may be a change of plan.'

'She's not just a witness isn't she? She's a suspect,' Tara Saunders said.

Sally thought it better not to answer that. She took the notebook back to the car and called Collins.

'And?' he asked.

'Exactly where you said. How on earth did you know?'

'Like father, like daughter. Robert hid the evidence of his crime in the attic of Ulvercott instead of destroying it. I wondered if Bella had done the same.'

'You couldn't know she had it all written down!'

'Of course she had. She likes being clever, she needed to crow about it. Or are you telling me there is nothing incriminating in this at all?'

'I haven't looked yet.'

'You've got more self control than I would have in the circumstances.'

'I've sealed it in an evidence bag,' she said reproachfully. 'Sir, what do I do now? Even if I read it now and the diary *is* incriminating, it's not a strong case. If I bring her in and it all comes to nothing her father is quite capable of suing us for wrongful arrest or something.'

The truth was, Sally didn't feel comfortable arresting a minor on her own. Not even with the relentlessly competent Tara Saunders looking on. If they were going to do this, it would have to be exactly by the book, with the Youth Offending Team on standby and a lawyer as well as an appropriate adult.

'There is more evidence,' Collins said, following his own train of thought, 'I assume the girls at Overdene House wear uniform?'

'Yes, but Bella was wearing her own clothes when she was at Ulvercott.'

'But she wouldn't have when she came to pick up her hockey things that Friday.'

'I suppose. What are you getting at?'

'This uniform, does it include gloves for winter? Dark blue wool?'

Sally watched a couple of uniformed girls walk past, giggling.

'The scrap of fibre in the medicine box!'

'Exactly. The lab haven't been able to match it with any clothing in the house.'

'But if they match it with Bella's glove...'

'...we can at least place her in Victor's room,' he concluded, 'But you are right, we'd better collate the evidence and run this past the DCI before we move in.'

Sally went back into the school. 'Ms Saunders, does Bella know I am here today?'

'No, we thought it would cause too much excitement to tell her beforehand. If you leave now, she'll be none the wiser.'

Sally drove back to the station in an even more thoughtful mood than when she had left.

45

Bella

Extracts from the diary of Bella Farndale

November 18
'It's a pity that she's such a very silly girl.'
Those were his exact words. And of course that cow Nora said nothing to contradict him. Silly! I am a lot cleverer than Lecky or Tig. Or Mortimer, but that is not exactly difficult. There are things living under stones that are cleverer than Mortimer Farndale.
Of course grandfather always thinks he is the smartest person in the room. It's true most of the time, probably. But I'll show him. One day, I'll show him.

25 December
Christmas at Ulvercott. Ultra-boring. Except for one thing. Grandfather had dinner with us for once, and Eliza brought him his medicine at the table. He showed the pills to us and said he would be dead within days if he didn't take them. He said it like it was a joke, but it wasn't really. I didn't know he was that ill, no one ever tells me anything, I always have to find things out for myself. It's lucky that I like finding things out.

8 January
I had lunch with Lecky and Tig and Juliette today. They'd all noticed what grandfather said about his pills at Christmas,

and the twins were saying it would be the perfect murder method. They weren't serious, of course, they never are. But they may be right. I saw them, they were just little white pills. You'd only need to get hold of something similar, and he'd never know he hadn't taken them.

I looked, but paracetamol tablets are too large, and so are the hormone replacement ones mum takes which I'm not supposed to know about. But I'm sure I've seen something just right somewhere recently.

17 January
I nicked nearly a month's worth of the pill from Leanne Parker-Stanhope's bag today. She is always acting like she's everybody's mum, serves her right if she gets pregnant!
Now I just need to choose the right time...

25 January
We're all expected at Ulvercott next week for Granny Olivia's anniversary. I never even knew the woman, I don't see why I should go, and there's hockey on Saturday too. But dad insisted, so I'll have to go. Maybe this is the right moment? Absolutely everybody will be there, including the twins' boyfriends and my dreary cousin Juliette. So plenty of possible suspects, but also plenty of people to see things they shouldn't. I may need a more complicated plan.

29 January
I've told Saunders that I need to get my kit from Ulvercott. She's so suspicious! She wanted to know what I had been using since Christmas in that case, so I told her I borrowed Britt's stuff. Then I had to find Britt to make sure she got the story straight. But at least I've got permission to go to Ulvercott on Friday. The pills are in my sports bag. The

weather is cold, so no one will wonder if I wear gloves. Everything is ready.

30 January
It was one of those still winter days when the park looks like a film set, the sky so pale that it was almost white. The house was silent as well, although I knew there must be people around somewhere. Jacqueline was probably in the kitchen, too far away to hear the creak as I went up the wooden stairs. There was no one about on the first floor, and the old man was in his room, watching television. I could hear the opening tune of Sherlock – he has always liked clever people who are also a bit weird. I found the dispensing tray where it always is, in the cabinet in his dressing room. The lid opened with a click that sounded loud to me, but he couldn't have heard it over the sound of the TV. There were pink capsules in there, and the little white pills I was looking for. They looked even more like the ones I had brought with me than I'd hoped, and I was sure no one would notice the difference. It was so easy to swap them, it hardly felt special. While Sherlock played his violin I put the box back where it belonged and slipped out of the room again, and back downstairs.
I went out through the back, making a detour past the pond to approach the house again from the front. The bus had just dropped its passengers by the main gate, so with any luck it would look like I had only just arrived. Jacqueline opened the door for me when I rang the bell, and said everyone would be so glad to see me (although she says that to everybody who arrives at Ulvercott House). Now all I have to do is wait.
It was so easy.

31 January

5-1! I'd like to say we played really well but the other side were just pathetic.
There's just time to write this before dad comes to pick me up. No news from Ulvercott yet. I wonder if it will happen while I'm there?

10 February
A policewoman came to talk to me, she said it was just routine. They always say that, don't they? I told her that I didn't like grandfather much and didn't pretend to be sorry that he's dead. You always have to make sure that you mostly tell the truth. She asked me if I had seen anything suspicious on Friday, and I said I hadn't, except I couldn't resist putting in a little dig at Juliette.
Saunders was there as my appropriate adult. Appropriate adult! That's a laugh. As if anyone would tell the police anything with a teacher listening in. They must know it's useless.

17 February
They've arrested dad! Although mum says he is only helping with inquiries, and anyway, they don't suspect him of the murder. But she still won't tell me what it is about. Perhaps he's been embezzling. He likes to pretend business is running smoothly, but according to Olly he's been in trouble for a while now. That's an idea, maybe Olly will talk to me.

later
I called Olly, and he says the police have discovered that dad had a child with the au pair when he was still living at home and that the child could be Lecky's boyfriend Matt! Oliver sounded upset. I just think it's exciting. I wonder if the police

think my dad killed his dad to keep this a secret? They don't really seem to be getting anywhere.

20 February
*I'm going home for the memorial on Monday, so I called Lecky to ask how the investigation is going. Don't want any nasty surprises. She says the police seem pretty sure that the substitution must have happened on Friday – I wonder how they know. It makes the pool of suspects smaller. Perhaps I need to do something to divert suspicion from myself. They're bound to wonder about my visit sooner or later. If there is an attack on me, then they'll have to suspect one of the others.
Lecky also says that the female cop is in love with her nephew/ex-boyfriend. Weird.*

21 February
*Right, I've got everything planned. I looked up how to repair the brakes on a bike on YouTube, so I only need to do that in reverse.
I'd better not take this to Ulvercott, in case the police get it into their heads to search the whole place. And I may not be able to write for a bit anyway, so I'd better hide this again.*

Geronimo!

46

DS Holmes turned the page, but the rest of the notebook was blank.

'That's the last bit,' Collins said, 'She was in hospital the next day.'

Sally shook her head. 'She took an enormous risk. That fall could have been harmless, or it could have maimed her for life.'

'She convinced herself she needed to do it to make the investigation go where she wanted it to go.'

'All this, just to act in her own crime drama.'

'Not just that. There is also her sense of grievance at Victor. Remember Ms Saunders said she was emotionally immature. Her grandfather called her silly, and that hurt, because she was proud of being clever. So she taught him a lesson. She isn't capable yet of seeing things like that in proportion.'

'So it had nothing to do with Annabel's death, or Matt's birth, or Juliette's bitterness.'

'Nothing at all. Like her father, Bella was moving in her own egotistic little bubble.'

'She as good as told me, when I first spoke to her. It's always the third suspect,' Sally said. She felt very stupid now, although she really knew that they couldn't have known earlier. Bella had played the game too well.

'Yes, that was the other part. She enjoyed getting the better of us.'

Sally leafed through the diary again. 'Manipulative little so-and-so. She doesn't like anyone much, does she? Except perhaps Ursula. She never says anything negative about Ursula.'

'No. And that is one loose end I still have to tie up with a ribbon for DCI Graham. The possible accessory.'

Collins went to Ulvercott House, which felt strangely empty. Eden, who opened the door for him, said that Eliza and David had gone away to stay with her sister, and that Jacqueline was out. But Ursula was there and willing to talk to him.

'Ms Westmacott, did you know?' he asked, without preliminary.

'No, I didn't know, Inspector, not for sure. But I suspected. I know them all, you see. As if they were my own. Victor always tried to impress on them all how privileged they were, but children don't really listen, do they? They are spoiled, all of them. And Bella the worst of the lot. She has a good brain, but nothing to use it on. I could imagine her doing something like this, out of some childish sense of resentment. I had almost made up my mind to speak to you about it. But then she was attacked herself, and I was actually relieved. If she knew something that would also explain why she was being so secretive, I could just imagine her hugging the knowledge to herself. I thought the attack let her off the hook.'

'But you spoke about your suspicions to Adam Rokeby *after* the attack,' Collins said, trying to get the sequence of events straight in his head.

'No, before.'

'Then what—? No, I'm sorry that is none of my business.'

'Then why did I ask to see him last Wednesday? You are right, that is none of your business. But I suppose I had better tell you, before you draw the wrong conclusions. One reason for me to be worried about Bella was that I will not be around to look after her much longer. I have six months, maybe a year to live, or so the specialists at the infirmary tell me.'

'I am sorry to hear that.'

She took a deep breath. 'I am not in pain. I am already older than Victor lived to be. I do not mind so much, for myself. But to have to leave the children... I know I shall have to tell them soon, but I don't want any fuss. I'm afraid I used Adam Rokeby as a kind of dry run. He is a good listener.'

'And that is also why you talked to Ms Krupinska.'

'Exactly. When the time comes I would like to have someone familiar to look after me.'

She put her palms to her temples. 'So much to think about. I wonder if Oliver will allow me to stay on here? I really cannot be moving house, on top of everything else.'

So that was why Mortimer had noticed his aunt acting oddly. She was preoccupied with her own problems. Adam Rokeby had been right, not everything was about murder.

'Thank you for telling me, Ms Westmacott. I promise we'll soon leave you alone. But you were telling me about Bella.'

'Yes, I thought the attack meant that I was wrong, and that someone else must be to blame for Victor's death. But then I started to think about that accident. It wasn't unusual for Bella to use the mountain bike trail, she knew it well. What I found strange was that she surely must have used her brakes on the way there. If they were cut, why did they only fail on that particular descent? But you got there before me.'

'Because she knew. She planned the accident herself.'

'Exactly. My poor, clever child.'

She straightened up and made a visible effort to collect herself. 'Was there anything else, Inspector?'

'No, that was all. Thank you for your help, Ms Westmacott. And I'm sorry.'

He closed the door of the incident room behind him and went downstairs, where he found Eden Kingston by the back door, talking to Oliver Farndale again.

'You'd have to contact the agency,' he heard her say.

'I will then. So, er. Goodbye, I suppose,' Oliver said, and walked away to where his car was parked.

They stood looking after him together.

'Today's my last time here,' Eden said, 'But he asked me if I'd come and work at Ulvercott if he opens the place for weddings and such. I told him he'd have to go through Odd Jobs. I don't suppose he will,' she added glumly.

'You don't think there may be hope for him yet?' he asked her.

'Not while he's hitched to Miss Perfect Planning, there isn't.' She gave him a properly thunderous look, then made a weak effort to cheer up. 'Oh, you must think I'm an awful minx. I'm not as bad as that, really.'

'Not even in a good cause?'

'You think it's worth a try?'

Collins thought of Oliver's enthusiasm, which only put in an appearance in the absence of Poppy Alexander, and nodded encouragingly. 'Go on, cause a little mayhem.'

Suddenly she set her shoulders, fluffed up her curls (*au naturel* today) and smiled broadly. 'Just watch me.' She set off down the path at a determined stride. 'Hey, Oliver! Hold up, man. Not finished talking to you.'

Collins left them to it and made his way to the main gates.

Back at the station he found Sally in the CID room removing the details of the Farndale case from the whiteboard.

'What will happen to her?' she asked, as she wiped out Bella's name along with her aunts and uncles.

'I'm not sure. We cannot prove that her actions actually led to Victor's death, you know what Dr Nakamura said. But her diary should at least be sufficient to get her psychiatric treatment.'

'She could argue that it was all just a fantasy,' Sally said sceptically. 'There's plenty who'd believe it of a teenage girl.'

'She could have argued that right up until the moment she put herself in mortal danger by riding a bicycle downhill without brakes. Dress that up any way you like, it wasn't the action of a sane person.'

'I don't suppose they are a very sane family,' his colleague concurred gloomily.

He thought he understood why she sounded so miserable. As far as he was concerned, the Farndales were over and done with. It was a little more complicated for Sally.

'Are you seeing Matt again?'

'I'd like to. I think he'd like to. But then he is a Farndale now, and I'm the one who collared his sister. God, it doesn't sound any more likely when you say it out loud. Bella is *his sister*.'

'He's much too sensible to hold that against you.'

'Yes, he is sensible, isn't he? I'm holding on to that thought.'

'I agree it all hangs together,' DCI Graham said, when Collins presented their case in the CID room the next morning, 'But how on earth did you get there?'

'Bella was trying to incriminate someone else, just like the twins were doing, but she was a lot more convincing. But once I realised that everything we had against Juliette rested on Bella's statements...'

'That's still quite a leap, though. After all, the twins were innocent even though they behaved in the same way.'

'Yes, there was more,' Collins conceded. 'It was something Sally said early on, asking what kind of murderer would use a method with only a middling chance of success. The answer is one to whom the challenge is more important than the outcome. And if there was one thing that was clear it was that Bella was enjoying the investigation immensely. Matt mentioned that, the first time we spoke. So did Simon Danvers, in his journal. The outsiders could see that it wasn't healthy. It took the family longer to see. We still haven't got a statement from Bettina, by the way. She's gone AWOL.'

'But Bella was attacked herself,' DC Robbins interrupted.

'No. She cut her own brakes, walked her bike to the top of the hill in Ulvercott Park, and rode down it wanting to stage an accident. I think she hadn't intended to be thrown off the bike for real, but it all played into her hands. It looked like someone had it in for Bella Farndale, and on top of that she got to stay at Ulvercott and watch us run around in circles.'

47

Bettina

to: sallyholmes2@mailspace.com
from: bettina@farndalemckinley.co.uk
re: apologies

Dear Sally,

I hope I may call you that now, although I'm writing to you in your capacity as a police officer.
I have heard that you and your colleagues have been looking for me, that I need to make a statement about Bella. Don't worry, I haven't disappeared, and I'll come to the station as soon as I'm feeling better. I had to get away from Ulvercott House, or I would have drowned in it all. I'm at the little flat in London my husband knows nothing about, my insurance in case the company heads south.

Last week, I learned that my husband abandoned his newborn child before he married me. I cannot pretend, after twenty-three years of marriage, to like Robert much, but I thought I knew him. It turns out that I did not. As soon as he was released on bail I told him I wanted a divorce. I haven't told his siblings that, they have other things on their minds, but I am determined. I cannot live with a man who would do that to a child, even though Matt Fielding turned out well, all things considered. I can see a little of Robert in him. Only physically, though. He is obviously a much nicer person. You are lucky.

A few days after my husband's arrest his brother was accused of assault. I had not been paying attention to the news, with everything that was happening at Ulvercott, so it came as a complete surprise to hear that there was a gang terrorising people in the town centre, and that Mortimer was one of them. When I heard, I comforted myself with the idea that my children would never do something like that.
What a fool I was.

Two days ago, I learned that my daughter is a murderer. I did not want to believe it. Of course she's not, I said to the inspector, you are mistaken, it's all circumstantial. I know all the right phrases. Haven't I heard them time and again, watching TV with Bella and Victor? Then he showed me her diary, and I could no longer lie to myself. I was there when she was arrested, I wanted her to know I will always be there, whatever she's done. But it was hard, she was like a stranger to me, walking between you and Ms Saunders with that empty look on her face.
I do not know my husband, I do not know my daughter. All that is safe and familiar is gone. I do not love my husband, but I do love my daughter. I have to believe that she is not evil, only young, mistaken. I have to believe that she can learn that she was wrong to do what she did. I wish Victor was still here to teach her that.
Until he was gone, I never realised that it was Victor who made us all into a family, who created that feeling of belonging. His children and grandchildren, their partners, different as we all are, we were all part of it. Now that he's

gone, we can see ourselves for what we are. Weak, avaricious, violent, vain. Misguided.

I must remember that I've still got my son, that Oliver is all right. He's young and bright and resilient, and he will get through this. We will get through this. Although right now I don't see how.
Nora and Sunita have asked me to come and stay with them for a while, and I think I'll accept. It was so kind of them, I almost cried. I must remember that people are still kind, that not everything is lost. I need to be strong for Oliver, for Ursula who was always so fond of my daughter, for the others who have suffered. Can we really still be a family after all this?

Sally, I promise you will get a proper statement from me as soon as I can be more coherent than this. And after that, I hope I shall see you again with Matt. Victor would have wanted that.

Yours,

Bettina McKinley

48

When Owen came home Dominic was in the study, at his desk. Behind him a long-legged black cat was stepping daintily on the rug and sniffing a chair leg.

'What are *you* doing here?' he asked, astonished.

'Hm? I live here.' Dominic looked up from his screen. 'Oh, you mean the cat. A woman called Jacqueline Whyatt brought him round. She says he is house-trained and eats something called Scrumbles. I understood from her that you two were already acquainted.'

'Well, yes. Hello, Foundling.'

The cat deigned to acknowledge him with a single head-bump against his ankle, then continued its exploration of the room.

'I do know him, but I wasn't aware that I had agreed to adopt him.'

Dominic closed his laptop. 'The Whyatt woman offered to take him away again when she realised you don't live on your own. I think she was trying to cheer your lonely existence. Anyway, he looks a politely raised kind of beast, it seemed churlish to refuse him houseroom.'

'You don't mind?'

'Do you want to keep him?'

'Yes.'

'Then I don't mind.'

Foundling looked up briefly at what his new humans were doing, decided it had nothing to do with him, and curled up on a sunny patch on top of *The Times Atlas of the World*.

Sally had asked Matt to come round, as casually as she could. Bella was in custody, the case was over and done, she had a reasonable human being as a boss again, but she still felt uneasy. Working as a detective you developed a sense for when there was something wrong with a story, and there was one thing in the Farndale saga which still bothered her. And she knew there was only one person who could help her clear it up.

'Matt?' she said, while setting the table in anticipation of a delivery meal.

'What's the matter?' he said, pausing in his attempt to get the foil off the screwcap of a supermarket red.

'It wasn't chance, was it? You knew all along you were connected to the Farndales, you knew long before you showed up at the station.'

He gave her a rueful smile. 'How did you know?'

It was Sally's turn to smile. 'Electra. I may not have seen you for twelve years, but I believe I know you well enough to know that she is really *not* your type.'

'Right. Of course, when it started I didn't think the whole affair would be subject to police scrutiny.'

'But how did you find out, if Victor only learned of your existence last month?'

He poured them both a glass of the red.

'I didn't find out so much as suspect. About two years ago I read an article in the Messenger about the re-opening of the Farndale Museum. There was a bio of Victor, with a black and white photo from when he was in his twenties. He looked familiar. And he had grown up in St Bride's, it was like a weird echo of my own life. Or, seeing as I came later, it was as if my life was an echo of his. I started to gather more information about him, anything I could find. Sometimes I thought I was on a wild goose chase. But then

I would see that likeness again. Obviously at that point I thought it was Victor who was my father.'

She looked at him with half-closed eyes, trying to find similarities with the Farndales. A hint of Nora in the nose, perhaps. And of course he was tall like his father. But it was hardly a striking likeness. 'It's strange that no one else saw the resemblance, though.'

'Not really. I have my mother's colouring, and Victor had light brown hair before he got bald. Ursula was the only member of the family old enough to recall what Victor looked like in his twenties, but why would she look for him in her niece's fiancé? There were enough times when I myself thought I had imagined the resemblance. But it wouldn't let me go.'

'And so you thought you'd start a relationship with a woman you believed to be your half-sister, just to get closer to her family.'

She might not like Electra much, but no woman deserved to be deceived like that.

Matt put down his glass. 'Is that what you think of me? She was in on it, Sal. She's not as stupid as you think, I could never have misled her like that. We were never in a relationship.'

'Okay, now you *have* surprised me.'

The doorbell rang, and she took the paper bag and paid the delivery-girl automatically, just wanting to get back to the kitchen and Matt's story.

'So you and Electra were never really together?' she asked, dumping the paper bag on the table.

Matt started to unpack it.

'It was all an act. We did meet at the fundraiser by chance, just as I told you. I told her my life story. Said I wondered if I had some connection to her family. She suggested I could get to know them all better if I posed as her boyfriend. It was just a lark to her. And I think when it looked like Tig and Simon were getting serious, she didn't want to be left behind. A fake boyfriend was better than none. We even made up the break-up story beforehand.'

'And when she and Antigone decided that you or Simon would make a good scapegoat for Victor's murder, was that also play-acting?'

'No, that was all true. Electra may not be as stupid as you think, but she is as ruthless. When she thought Tig or Mortimer could be in danger she threw me to the wolves without a second thought. Eat your biryani, it's getting cold.'

Sally did as she was told, but she was still thinking about what she had just learned.

'So by the time Collie asked you to go back to Ulvercott you were acting that you were acting being together,' she concluded.

'Exactly. Do you think he knows, the inspector?'

'He hasn't said anything. But it is very difficult for people who are guilty of something not to protest too much, and Owen usually picks up on it. He knew Gareth Swift was a wrong'un right from the start, long before we connected him to the Butcher's Row gang.'

'A wrong'un? Do you really call them that?'

'We do. Or crooks, or villains, or, you know, just plain criminals. None of which you are. I'm glad I know everything now. I *do* know everything now?'

He clinked his glass against hers. 'You know as much as I do.'

And that would have to be enough.

Author's note

Readers of Agatha Christie will not have been surprised by the identity of the murderer in this story: *After St Bride* is my bow to the Queen of Crime.

The story of how Jake Danvers met Noah Rosenthal and embarked on his writing career is told in the novella *The Gift*, which is not a mystery and so not really part of the series.

Printed in Dunstable, United Kingdom